RYAN AUSSIE SMITH

Thorn

Shadow's Lament Book One

AUTHORTUNITIES

First published by Authortunities Press 2026

Second edition

ISBN: 978-1-959048-21-3

Editing by Angela Yuriko Smith

This book was professionally typeset on Reedsy.
Find out more at reedsy.com

Contents

Children's talent to endure stems from their ignorance of alternatives.
Maya Angelou

Twisted Shoots

The chilling voice was in his ear again, whispering secret truths across an acid-tipped tongue. Truths of history, deceit and of course his birthright. These midnight visits had increased as of late for the shadowy figure. The boy lying below was completely unaware as his head was filled with the knowledge kings and emperors would kill to possess. *Some truths were hard to bear and troubled the boy, beads of sweat formed on his brow and the sound of teeth grinding was faintly audible in the still room. However, the shadow did not care, could not care. Necessary evils were exactly that, necessary. The child required education and the world was a painful place. Inside the boy's head were visions of pain, death and destruction. The stench of burning flesh filled his nostrils and the sound of battle cries rang in his ears.*

In utter silence, Thorn awoke to a darkened room. Swallowing enormous gulps of air, his heart thundered in his ears with the repetitious rhythm of a war drum. Thorn had trained himself to stop the instinctual screaming when the nightmare nights came. The other Viridio children already considered him an outcast without the need for more of his unusual activity. Some part of him feared the dreams were not showing him the past, but preparing him for a future he had no wish to inherit.

The cool night air licked at Thorn's dampened skin as he turned into a sitting position. It chilled his spine but did little to clear the thick molasses of thoughts clouding his mind. Head slumping into shaking hands, Thorn sat in a meditative state until the first trickles of light parted the dense canopy overhead.

The shaking in his hands slowly dissipated, replaced with a familiar sense of morbid curiosity. Who were the people in these dreams and what did they do to deserve such a fate? Were they real or was he just as much of an oddity as everyone thought? Individualism was shunned within the Viridio, generic thinking was a must. To possess a mind capable of idealistic thoughts and curiosity that willed action was seldom seen, if not completely lacking in the forest. Thorn was therefore called unusual, strange and dangerous by all he knew. For what other way could the eternal children of the forest survive the centuries without infighting and war? These children were the sons and daughters of the nymphs, malevolent beings that lured men to their death with irresistible siren song.

The playful nature of these energetic beauties masked their darker purpose. The bones of thousands could be found scattered throughout the forest. Adventurers, traders, marauders—all had fallen under the sensual spell of these immortals and drifted off to eternal sleep. Nature never wastes and every death brought a new life to the village. The nymphs relied on wayward travelers to produce their children. Their offspring obtained the immortality and youthful beauty of their mothers but never reached the age of puberty. They also obtained traits from their fathers, bringing a slight sense of diversity to the population. Contact with the mothers was minimal but they did sometimes visit their offspring, floating in as they slept to sing soothing lullabies or to leave presents of berries and exotic substances. By sunrise, however, there would be naught but pleasant memories and gifts. None had ever communicated with the nymphs and it was forbidden to try. So it was that the Viridio raised themselves upon the knowledge of those that came before and so it was that the ignorance of the forest continued.

Piercing blue eyes sliced through the haze of early morning as Thorn stood on the supporting branch of his own tree dwelling. Keen observation made it clear that not a single soul within Tsanie was stirring. The village of trees was his, for now. Swinging beneath the enormous branch, Thorn caught hold of the rope ladder beneath and began his descent. The enormous tree on which his dwelling sat was a great source of venerated love within the Viridio community. It was one of four trees within the entire forest that could provide a clear view of life above the tree canopy. Thorn was lucky enough to be one of the tree's inhabitants. Lucky was perhaps not the ideal term to describe his current lodgings, however.

Thorn. It was an ugly name not like Azalea, Marinoth or Milia but it was not his choice. Nymphs were not particular as to where they left their newborn offspring, and the Viridio had adopted the custom of choosing names based on birth surroundings. Whether it is a bed of soft yellow Milia flowers or a fresh bushel of spearmint, each new Viridio became part of the forest in name and spirit.

On the day of Thorn's birth it was said that the earth shook and fires scorched half of the forest. That same day a nymph brought a Viridio child into existence, but died in the process, something that had never happened before. Next to the deceased creature lay a weeping newborn Viridio child cradled in a hammock of blackened thorns. Thorn was that unlucky child, and it was because of his unprecedented birth that many of the Viridio perceived him as cursed and of unclean nature. He was therefore barely tolerated in the beginning and, even now, kept at a safe distance. Given residence on the Grand Tree, Thorn slept far up in the canopy, because of their fear.

The descent could be long and tiresome in the summer, but during the winter when the rivers ran high it became the best part of his day. One such river now flowed deep and swift a short distance from the grand tree, and the long rope ladder on which Thorn now clung. A grin of mischievous delight formed on the forest boy's face as he began swinging back and forth. The rhythmic swing arced further and further, sending shock waves to the top and bottom of the ladder. Looking like a giant sea serpent, the ladder now had enough force behind it and Thorn took position. Using the power of the ladder's momentum, he launched himself into the air. The fleeting silence of the forest was quickly replaced with the deafening roar of the wind passing over his ears. The small torches burning outside tree dwellings flashed past as Thorn gained speed in his fall. The river that was once distant charged towards him as he hurtled towards it.

Thorn's feet hit the water with a jolt, and then the entire world was engulfed in white foam and bubbles. He plummeted towards the darkness below until riverbed rocks met his searching feet. All movement ceased in the cool darkness, and for a few seconds Thorn turned off his mind, focusing on the flowing water. It helped wash away the thoughts of death that still lingered from his dreams, and the cold temperature of the river brought him to the present moment. Kicking off of the rocks, Thorn torpedoed his way to the surface.

Gulping a huge lungful of air, Thorn glided towards the water's edge, content that he had not made enough noise to wake the other Viridio. He did not want any of them to see the direction he would be traveling today, or suspicion would be ripe. Climbing up the roots of a nearby tree, Thorn pulled himself out of the water. His green and brown tunic was mottled to blend with the forest. From the waterlogged material columns of liquid cascaded to the damp soil beneath his feet. This was of no concern, however, as the distance Thorn had to cover during the morning would dry his clothes quickly. Working his way towards Topside Grove, Thorn dashed from tree to tree, keeping his feet quiet and his presence unknown. Arriving at Milia's dwelling, Thorn rolled a rock to the side revealing the rabbit skin satchel he had left there the week before. Milia did not know of Thorn's little stash next to her house, but she would not have cared even if she did. Regardless of her supporting nature, she wasn't well known for keeping secrets under pressure. Thorn anticipated pressing questions should he return late today. Questions were constantly thrown at her about Thorn's activities, and he had opted to play this adventure safe and avoid arousing curiosity.

Milia was the closest thing to a friend Thorn had known in his 222 years of life. He had, to some extent, corrupted her. For her, their association had stripped away the blind loyalty to the ones who came before and encouraged her individualistic thought. Fortunately, due to her youthful age and rosy demeanor, the others had not shunned her as they did him. A fact Thorn was grateful for. It was selfish for him to befriend her, but she seemed more intent on the relationship than he did, so he had given up trying to push her away.

The leaves whipped at Thorn's face while sweat poured down his back. Sprinting through the forest was tough work, but distance was needed in the morning before the heat of the day hit. Dodging through the trees and diving over rocks with the fluid movement of a two-century-old forest dweller, he did not so much see the forest as he felt it. His satchel was heavy with the items he had accumulated and made this particular trip a tiresome one. Every item, however, had its purpose and would be needed when he reached his destination. Slowing down to a walk, Thorn seized the water skin hanging loosely from his waist and brought it to his lips. He had been running at a constant speed all morning and knew the midday heat would mark the proximity to his destination. He wanted to arrive well rested so he could immediately enter and get to work.

The morning dew was still evident on many of the leaves in this part of the forest, and the lack of air movement was obviously the cause. Thorn had discovered, in his travels, that the further he went from the forest's center the closer the trees became. It was almost as if the trees had focused their efforts to deter and slow any potential trespassers, creating a makeshift wall of bark and leaves that spanned for miles. As Thorn made his winding way through the trees, he once again remembered why he had run so long without rest. The air was so thick in this section of the forest that traveling at walking pace took as much effort as running, although running through the trees at least gave the impression of a breeze.

The light of the morning sun was now visible in the distance, and Thorn knew he would soon be in the Forbidden Meadow which housed the Temple of Death. The Viridio thought it appropriate to name outlawed areas of the forest outrageously forbidding names to quell any thought of investigation. It had taken Thorn almost 50 years of life for his curiosity to get the better of him. His first excursion had been very short and bland, but the simple act of rebelling thrilled him more than anything that had come before. For over a century, he had traveled to these forbidden zones in search of excitement, adventure, knowledge—basically anything to break up the tedious routines of Viridio life. The first time Thorn had traveled to one of the temples, it was nothing more than a ruin. Crumbling stone, half reclaimed by the forest, vine-covered walls and dilapidated wooden structures made the once impressive structure look small and unimposing. Only when studying the temple in greater detail was the architectural magnitude revealed. The temples were mazes of rooms and hallways—heavily booby-trapped rooms and hallways. Recently Thorn found an intact temple which stood the test of time and was not a decaying wreck. For the past 5 years he had been attempting to learn its secrets, enjoying the challenge it posed. Each room presented a particular test for body and mind. Without excellent reflexes and an understanding of the temple structures, death was an inescapable certainty.

The temple was visible long before the trees gave way to an expanse of lush meadow, looming in the distance like an enormous intruder. It was a disheveled monstrosity of carved stone, polished metal, wood and marble, clearly out of place in otherwise virgin landscape. It was as if the building had rolled across the land, collecting diverse sections of houses, huts and palaces. A beautiful white marble pillar would adorn a dilapidated sheet metal wall, crudely etched slate steps would end abruptly in a smooth clay dome with a painted landscape of meticulously detailed animals prancing about. Grotesque stone creatures adorned the walls and pillars, but were clearly from different regions, some looking majestic in their fury whilst others were the things of twisted nightmares. The mismatched jumble of architecture rose in this confused manner until it towered over the enormous trees surrounding it. Thorn strolled calmly through the trees, eyes fixed on his target and goal. He was determined. He would puzzle out all its secrets today or die trying.

It seemed he wasn't the only one fixated on the temple. It was as if the entire forest led to it, the forest floor gently tilting that way with a downhill slope, coaxing travelers with an easy walk. Well-worn animal trails led to the temple, despite their apparent lack of use. Spider webs, rocky outcrops and fallen trees never barred the path towards the temple, but any path leading away would quickly become difficult. Thorn believed that the forest wanted people to find the temple and test their skills within. It was either that, or the temple was another defense of the forest. Any outsiders that somehow managed to elude the nymphs and made it this far into the trees would be tired from days of traveling. A downhill slope, coupled with unfamiliar surroundings and exhaustion, would make the path of least resistance very desirable.

The funneling effect of the meadow made it a landmark of note in the northern forest. Exuding an unseen force, stumbling too close to the temple had one result. Even knowing its power it still required considerable effort to break free from its vortex of influence as Thorn had learned quite well. The temple's grand stature and oddity fed visions of wealth and power within its walls. Inside, the life-threatening traps constructed to ward off intruders did little more than feed the temptation, making the occasional explorer more determined. The bones of countless adventurers could be found impaled, crushed and charred by the wide variety of traps.

The remains were all from the tall race of man, creatures from outside the forest's boundaries. Thorn dreamed of them regularly, but had never met one face-to-face. It intrigued him that the men threw their lives away so readily for the mere possibility of treasure when they were wearing it as clothing. Dust covered metal tunics with matching gloves, greaves and boots lay unaffected among the decaying bones of their former masters. Pouches of precious metals lay scattered on the floor where their owners had fallen. Glittering jewelry with red, blue and clear stones adorned skeletal hands and hung loosely on drying rib cages.

Unfortunately, these foolish travelers often chose to expire in the most inconvenient locations, and retrieval of their personal effects was near impossible. The personal treasures held only fleeting desire for Thorn, however. No vendor he knew would barter for possibly cursed foreign objects, and he would have to double in physical size to even consider wearing the clothing. Strange treasures from beyond the boundaries were something to gather for curiosity, but never to share. He had learnt his lesson long ago and would not have it repeated. Thorn suspected the shiny metal clothing was insignificant compared to the treasures that lay within the temple, treasures that he would soon possess.

Dancing Axes and Spiral Blades

Standing in silence, Thorn placed his satchel on the ground and filled his lungs with the temple's stale air. It smelled of mold, dust and age, the epitome of stale, and this was just the first room. Thorn knew it would become much denser the deeper he traveled. Thorn closed his eyes for a moment to focus his heightened vision and senses. The temple interior revealed itself as another world when his eyelids snapped open again.

Five separate passages presented themselves before Thorn in a perfect line. He had discovered from his previous expeditions that all but one were decoys, constructed to misdirect all who would seek the temple's secrets. Running the length of all five corridors had earned him nothing but cuts, bruises and a night spent unconscious. The dusty marble floor had become his impromptu sleeping quarters when a sizable rock projectile had knocked him unconscious. As luck would have it, Thorn awoke staring directly at the ceiling, or more accurately at a panel of the ceiling that was missing. This missing panel provided Thorn with access to higher levels of interlinking passages.

Strolling down the correct passageway, Thorn rummaged through his pack until his hand fell upon tough strips of leather made from the scaled skin of the chained back dragon lizard. Wrapping the long strips around his hands several times, the scales would provide excellent protection from the barbed vines he would soon be climbing. Approaching the missing panel, Thorn reached for the ropy vines that hung limply from the ceiling. Several older thorns crunched in his hand as he hauled himself up the wall and towards the dark square looming overhead.

Once within the ceiling cavity, the temple opened up to become a three-dimensional maze. The twisting hallways doubled back on themselves, confusing the eyes and the mind. Shining mirrored surfaces reflected a perfect image of hallways that were not actually there. Any movement he made was replicated multiple times in the mirrors, making him feel like he was not alone. Thorn took off at a jog, once again reaching into his satchel to produce a small map carved into flexible tree bark. Following the etchings on the bark, Thorn traversed through the convoluted maze of hallways. There was no sound save the echoing of his feet padding across the damp moss. His path led him up, down, left-low, left-high, right twice and then through yet another ceiling hatch. Thorn ran through the maze, glancing at his map, until a shining gleam of sweat glistened on his brow.

The acrid smell that suddenly assaulted Thorn's nostrils indicated he was almost through the maze. The alcove ahead dripped with thick yellow tears whilst clouds of noxious spores made the air shimmer like a mirage. Thorn knew the tight hallway would open up into a larger room, past the dripping alcove, and here an invisible danger lurked.

Rummaging for a cloth pouch stitched in the satchel's lining, Thorn's hand returned with a fistful of charcoal-colored nuts. Misspheri nuts were a rarity, even amongst the Viridio, due to their plant's delicate nature and slow growth cycle. Appearing only in the fastest moving and clearest streams, the Misspheri plant would produce only a single nut each year. These nuts were greatly valued due to their healing properties, but in Thorn's hands they served a much different purpose. Each nut had a natural hole through its center. When placed in the mouth, the air that was sucked through that hole was filtered of all toxins. The natural absorbance of the nuts made this possible.

Before placing one of the nuts between his lips, Thorn inhaled until his lungs burned, and at a slow, relaxed pace he made his way toward the next room. Stinging tears filled his eyes as he trudged his way past another enormous Peupolis mushroom as it belched continuous clouds of yellow gas into the air. The gas was known as The Living Insanity. When inhaled, it caused hallucinations, the inability to think and partial paralysis. In high enough doses, the infected also had the nasty habit of clawing their skin off.

The sheer number of Peupolis mushrooms caused the air to shimmer and twist. The toxicity of the fumes spewing out created a world of burning senses and confusion. Anyone caught breathing in this room would not continue to do so for long. Thorn made his way calmly through the clumping of mushrooms towards one of the far corners of the room. Dropping his current breathing nut to the damp stone floor, he exhaled slowly and placed another between his lips. A towering wall appeared out of the distorting fumes, and raising one arm, Thorn placed a hand on it. Walking parallel to the wall, Thorn relied on his sense of touch to lead him rather than his eyes. He had closed them some time ago, yet they still streamed with clumping, yellow tears. The surface of the wall changed from wet stone to a coarse cloth material, signaling the time to push. Propping his shoulder against the panel, Thorn strained forward until there was an audible click. A muffled rumbling sound reverberated across the large room.

The stone slabs ground across one another noisily as Thorn relaxed to conserve air. Based on past experience, the slab would take some time to move and time was working against him in this room. Slowing his heart beat, Thorn forced himself into a meditative state, receding from the searing pain of his eyes to draw focus from the loud and slow throbbing residing in his chest and ears. Waiting for lungs to scream for oxygen, Thorn would return to the world only to replace the Misspheri nuts that were now diminishing in supply.

Time dragged on, and the grinding sound continued its long slow growl. Waiting patiently, Thorn pictured the door across the room in his mind. A small opening that would quickly close the moment he lessened the pressure on the cloth plate. Last time Thorn had attempted this obstacle, the door had almost taken off his foot as it slammed behind him. This time would not be so close. The grinding stopped, and a loud clanking sound reverberated beneath Thorn's fingertips. It was time.

Taking one last drag from an unused nut, Thorn propelled himself off of the wall, sprinting for the fast closing door hidden behind the toxic fumes. Ducking and weaving as if he was in the forest again, Thorn ran blindly through the fumes, narrowly missing the large mushrooms that only became visible when he was almost slamming into them. His heart pounded in his ears from lack of oxygen and his vision became spotted, as if he had recently been staring at the sun. Through the vapors, the dark door became visible as it dropped fast from the ceiling. Throwing himself forward in a dive, Thorn skidded on his stomach through the doorway as it slammed with a deafening crash behind him. Lifting himself up, immediately Thorn ran without releasing his breath. He needed to gain distance from the door and the fumes that had seeped through it. Glancing over his shoulder, Thorn concluded that he was far enough and collapsed on the floor panting erratically. Sucking dusty air into his lungs never felt so good, even if his lungs were stinging from the overuse they had endured.

After emptying the contents of his water skin onto his burning face and eyes, he lifted himself from the floor. The corridor he now found himself in was much brighter than the previous ones. However, unlike the previous room dripping with liquid air, this corridor was nice and dry. Thorn's current attire was soaked with stagnant water and had absorbed enough of the fumes to render them unusable. Unbuttoning his tunic, Thorn peeled his clothing off, throwing it to the floor with a moist slap. Toweling himself down with a rag from his satchel, he took special care to remove any moisture on or around his face. The mushrooms' toxin was only truly dangerous if inhaled, but should a drop of it find its way to his mouth, the resulting hour would not be fun.

Grabbing an assortment of spare clothing, it was thoroughly inspected before use. Donning his new attire, Thorn contemplated his next move. Next, he would enter the room with the dropping floor and pit spikes which required the rope he had packed. After this, it was straight through the corridor of dancing axes and spiral blades. All of these, however, would be child's play in comparison to the dart room. The only obstacle Thorn was yet to overcome, and the most dangerous. Snapping himself out of morbid daydreams, Thorn stopped contemplating his looming demise and decided to get moving. There was no point thinking about the dangers until they were upon him. The fun would soon begin.

Through the Maze

The darts exploded from walls like a swarm of angry hornets. Hundreds of tiny projectiles, impossible to see, hissed past Thorn's tumbling body as he threw himself to the left. Tucking into a ball he rolled, narrowly avoiding the barrage before he was once again hurtling down the corridor. In one fluid motion, his body twisted, tumbling head over feet to miss a tripping wire. Each footfall was accompanied by the sound of hundreds of deadly darts erupting from the walls. Thorn's muscles burnt and strained to continue the pace, but every step required instant and primitive evasion to remain alive. The constant battering of rolls and dives would soon come to an end as he quickly approached the point of no return. Body tilted at a diagonal, the darts whipped by, inches from his exposed neck, as Thorn chanced a look at his target. The wall of faces materialized out of nowhere, he had never seen it so close. Hundreds of expression-filled faces, frozen in stone, watched as Thorn darted towards them. Be it an angry growl or a weeping sob, all faces had an open mouth and within, a dart-sized hole. The checkerboard face wall marked the end of the corridor and true danger. Speed was integral now more than ever as Thorn delved deep into his reserves of stamina preparing for the final obstacle.

A loud click reverberated through Thorn's right foot as the floor triggered. All darts stopped firing and the corridor fell silent, only the continuous thud of deer-skin boots and Thorn's heaving breath could be heard. Running directly at the wall, Thorn prepared his body for the jump. Launching up mid-stride, his foot slammed directly into the forehead of a saddened face. He glimpsed anguish and tears frozen in stone beneath his boot for a split second before momentum forced him upwards. Misjudging the force of impact, Thorn's knee jarred and twisted with a sickening pop. Ignoring the pain, he sprang off of the wall and straight towards the ceiling. Above, a small cylindrical hole was barely visible behind the vines that had masked its presence. Hands outstretched, Thorn grasped at the vines, barely reaching the lowest one with the tips of his fingers. Sinking his fingernails in, he scrambled into the hole with maddened fervor just as a deafening storm erupted below him.

Hanging with one hand from a vine within the shaft, he looked down on the carnage that he narrowly escaped. The corridor below was now thick with darts as every hole lining the walls fired continuously. Thorn was mesmerized at the sheer number of darts that filled the corridor and the screeching high-pitched scream they made as they shot from wall to wall. Almost every dart that fired disappeared into a hole in the adjacent wall. The architecture of the dart room was truly a marvel, conserving ammunition for years of protection. Thorn had anticipated the final pressure plate would spell death for the unaware, but nothing he had seen from previous temples could have prepared him for this.

Turning reluctantly from the angry hiss and enthralling sights below, Thorn began to climb. Satisfaction from overcoming yet another deadly obstacle was quickly replaced by his burning curiosity for what was to come. Favoring one leg as he climbed, Thorn continued up the vines into the deeper darkness of the vertical shaft. It did not take long until even Thorn's eyes could not penetrate the darkness and he was rendered blind. Touch and sound became his world, but vision was missed as his face continually met entangling vines. The shaft began to level out and the climb soon became a crawl. This freed his hands to dispatch the cumbersome vines barring his path. Hissing from the dart swarm in the previous room was faint yet still present and the growing pain in his left knee was a constant reminder of how close to death he had truly been.

Death was a fantastically taboo subject within the Village of Tsanie, and rightfully so. When dealing with immortals that had always known peace, the concept of dying was as inconceivable as sprouting wings and flying away. Thorn mused at the anger displayed when conversations had brushed the surface of that particular topic and the reprimands that followed. During this lapse of concentration, Thorn did not react when his hand reached out and felt nothing but air. His body had already tumbled forward as desperate hands scrabbled to grab a ledge, vine or anything to stop him from falling into this unknown hole. To his dismay, Thorn grasped at nothingness as he plummeted downwards. Bouncing off of the sides of the shaft, barbed vines whipped and snagged his clothing. They bit into his flesh, just enough to snap beneath his weight as the fall continued. Curling into a ball, Thorn tried to minimize the damage as demonic vines wrapped around his limbs, attempting to sever anything they touched.

Bursting out of the vine-infested shaft, light assaulted Thorn's eyes for the briefest of moments before the ground rushed up to meet him. The force of the stone floor's impact crushed his chest like a pancake and any air within exploded from his lungs. Ears still ringing, Thorn could barely hear the strange quivering noise that hummed unbidden from his bloodied lips. Blinking back tears and spotty vision he rolled to one side, trying to suck in air as the embarrassing humming continued. Small breaths started to fill his frozen lungs, returning feeling to his extremities. The numbness receded, but the shock of impact on his limbs lingered. A stabbing pain knifed its way through his joints as sensation returned but this was quickly forgotten. Its replacement came in the form of a maddening sting and itching sensation, settling on Thorn's skin like an enormous blanket of poison ivy. The impulse to scratch and tear at his skin like a rabid animal took considerable willpower to squelch but he resisted the urge.

Lifting the torn remains of his body up into a kneeling position, Thorn surveyed his surroundings. The gaping hole in the ceiling was higher than he had suspected based on the injuries suffered. Judging by the height and solid ground below, the fall could have been fatal had he not landed on his cushioned satchel. Painful as they were, the vines had also played a part, slowing his descent. It had, however, cost him and the price paid was the currency of flesh and blood. The evidence seeped forward as paper-thin nicks and cuts began to appear on his arms and chest, reddening his tunic.

His satchel had launched its contents quite a distance upon impact. His belongings now lay sprawled across the floor in a disheveled mess. Thorn's eyes adjusted to the brightened room. Beams of sunlight pierced their way through the darkness from small rectangular slits sliced in the stone walls. Thick layers of dust covered the floor; save for the patch Thorn had crashed down upon. His disturbance had caused the ancient layers to go puffing into the air around him. The resulting clouds sparkled and danced in the light beams, as if alive. Thorn found himself caught in a trance as he watched the ever-changing particles. Subconsciously moving towards one of the thin light beams, he reached out as if to touch it. The gnarled and bloody hand that caressed the air seemed so out of place. Jerking it back as if suddenly stung, Thorn was reminded of the ever-present danger that lurked around every corner. Within the Temple, everything seemed to misdirect and hide a deeper, generally harmful, purpose.

Taking time to really observe his surroundings, Thorn noticed an unusual change from the rest of the temple. Unlike its predecessors, this room lacked the chaotic nature and random scatter of mismatched architecture that was so prominent everywhere else. Small stone pedestals ran parallel to each wall in identical fashion and the obvious decay of every previous chamber was not evident here. From ceiling to floor, the symmetry of carved stone was so perfect it was unnerving. The muted gray overtones of dust accumulated over the centuries may have hidden any imperfections but the room was not completely covered and seemed in immaculate condition despite this.

Bending down, Thorn began herding his scattered items into the torn remains of his satchel. His caution of the light beams resulted in awkward shuffling steps and he was forced to abandon a few items that were out of reach. Slinging the pack over his shoulders, Thorn limped slowly towards one side of the chamber. Placing more pressure on his healthy leg, Thorn hobbled forward, grimacing with every step. Like a distrustful deer, he was poised for action, ready to dodge any danger that lurked in the unknown room. Smoky clouds puffed from the floor with every measured footstep whilst his eyes scanned left to right, searching for the death he was certain hid beneath the thick layers of dust. A splash of red in the gray gloom slowly became a door as

Thorn slowly trudged toward it. The enormous red door was soon towering over him with thick planks of a rosy red wood that crisscrossed the darker mahogany panels. Green veins tarnished the round silver handle that sat dead center of the door and filigree bands similarly aged climbed its sides like the rungs of a ladder. The ancient markings that had once held such splendor were reduced to smudged stains on the ancient red wood.

Thorn lent his weight on the door and surprisingly, it swung open with little resistance. Exhausted and bleeding, it took a moment for the realization to sink in. He had made it. Enormous hills of gleaming, bright treasure ringed the room sitting high on walls obscured from view. Twinkling like starlight in a darkened sky, diamonds, rubies, sapphires and emeralds reflected colorful shadows on stacked piles of shining coins. Silver and gold objects gleamed in the dim light untarnished by age. Jewel encrusted crowns, goblets and statues sat on the piles of gold and silver coins like ducks on a large lake. Thorn looked around with satisfaction and a strange sense of desire. Gold and jewels meant little and less to the Viridio, he knew this, yet the room filled with treasures still set his mouth to watering.

Bending to collect a handful of gold, Thorn collapsed under the weight of his damaged knee, landing face first in a treasure pile that felt like a slab of solid stone. Losing consciousness for a second, Thorn awoke when his knee throbbed suddenly from being held at a strange angle. Rolling over, he gingerly rolled the blood-soaked fabric of his trousers up, finally admitting there might be a problem. What had once been a knobby little knee attached to a skinny leg was now a purple hunk of swollen meat. Nothing appeared to be broken, but his knee joint was clearly damaged and almost unrecognizable behind the swelling. Covering up the purple appendage Thorn ran his hand over the coins, bringing up a handful of heavy gold and silver. Triangles, squares and disks, the coins were clearly from different regions. Faces and crude writing was stamped into the precious metal, but just as the temple itself, its treasures were mismatched and varied. Thorn let the coins trickle through his fingers before he heaved himself to his feet. There had to be something of greater value in this room apart from pretty stones and gold coins.

Following a small pathway that provided a valley through piles of gems, Thorn made his way deeper into the room of treasures. Towards what seemed like the center of the room, the mountains of gold parted, revealing an altar that stood alone and unadorned. Polished jet-black marble drew the eye away from the surrounding treasures that reflected on its mirrored surface. Moving closer, Thorn saw no seams in the stone, meaning it was carved out of a single block. The center was hollowed out to form an enormous bowl that was large enough for Thorn to sit in.

Hobbling up, Thorn placed his hands on the altar and leaned to peer down into the bowl. Disappointment ran through him when he saw it was empty. Stretching, Thorn reached low, running his fingertips along its smooth interior, trying to deduce what it could have held. This altar was so obviously significant in some way, and yet Thorn could not figure out how. Slumping against the altar, Thorn let his hands dangle above the bowl as he collected his thoughts. A single drop of blood that had been pooling on his elbow slowly snaked its way down his forearm. Making its way to Thorn's index finger it hung for a few seconds before the gathering mass released its hold, falling into the bowl below. Thorn watched it with disinterest, feeling vague self-pity at his broken body.

Without warning, lightning arced through his arms and Thorn was thrown ten feet backwards, slamming into a mound of gold metal disks. Gasping from breath and confused at what had just happened, Thorn noticed that the dark marble altar had brightened in color and the bowl in the center was steaming. The stone glowed with a white-hot fury, throbbing with light. Light, then dark, then light again, the pulse went on as steam rushed into the air. Thorn felt heat prickle his skin, but as the glow slowed its pulse, the light, heat and steam all stopped gradually, like a passing storm. Cautiously, Thorn moved back to the altar and without touching it attempted to peer into the hollow bowl. When this proved difficult, he tested its surface with taps of his fingers like you would a cooking pan. Concluding the altar was no longer charged, Thorn leaned over the hollow bowl and found himself staring at a sparkling dot at its center.

On closer inspection, the dot was a glittering sand-like substance that was clearly not present before the light and steam display. Thorn's curiosity was piqued; he began to understand why the altar had significance. Peeling off his torn tunic, Thorn gripped both ends and wrung out the blood and sweat that had soaked deep into the fabric. The paper-thin cuts had not gone deep, but their sheer quantity provided ample blood and as he twisted the tunic a sizable stream of liquid trickled into the altar's basin. Thorn took several steps back in anticipation and for a brief moment nothing happened.

"Perhaps it only works once," Thorn said out loud.

As the words left his mouth, the altar again flashed a blinding white and steam billowed from its center. It had turned into a miniature sun with a light so bright Thorn's closed eyelids did nothing to stop the glaring pain. Heat radiated from it with the intensity of a thousand forest fires and the ground began to shudder. The shaking loosened large stacks of gold coins that bounced and flipped across the floor whilst other piles of treasure collapsed, crashing loudly. Crawling away from the pain, Thorn burrowed into the closest mound of treasure, blanketing himself with a makeshift barrier. The mound above his head was threatening to topple as it wobbled violently with the tremors. The enormous release of energy continued its burning assault and as Thorn buried himself he could smell the hair on his legs burning.

Thorn was buried head to toe when the altar ceased its bellowing. The room took some time before it was comfortably cool again and even longer before Thorn trusted it to remain that way. No longer in danger, Thorn shimmied out of his hiding spot and inspected his body for burns. Apart from the melted loss of his leg hairs and a throbbing sensation in his feet, Thorn was no worse for wear, but the rest of the treasure room had not been so lucky. Anything within arm's reach of the altar had vaporized in the intense heat. Nearby metal disks were now pools of melted gold and silver. They made pinging sounds as they solidified in the cooling temperatures. A gold and jade statue that had once been a powerful looking man with three heads now looked like a half-used candle with drips forming stalactites beneath its platform. Fragments of gemstone which had been superheated to the point of fracture littered the floor, still warm to the touch.

Content that he hadn't melted like many of the gold disks around him,

Thorn made his way to the altar to inspect his handiwork. As expected, the altar had once again produced glittering white silver sand but this time there was a sizable amount. Fine sand that magically appeared from blood was something to bag up for further study, thought Thorn. Clutching his now empty water skin, Thorn scooped in greedy handfuls of the outwardly mundane substance and corked the opening when it was full to bursting. Reattaching the water skin to his belt, Thorn looked around at the well-cooked room where he now stood. Coins had melted to the floor and many gems still smoked and sizzled looking unstable. On one side of the room, an enormous pile of treasure had created a landslide, revealing a spectacularly complicated and advanced hidden door mechanism.

When scouting the dilapidated remains of other forest temples, Thorn had seen piles of scrap metal just like this mechanism. They had been broken rusted things with no conceivable purpose, but as Thorn turned the heavy hexagonal handle the mechanism's complexity revealed itself. The handle turned and the wall sprung to life. Gears spun in unison, lifting pulleys and twisting large spiked spokes. A chain clattered deep below the door's surface, spinning several dials towards the ceiling before four thick bolts slowly receded from each of the door's four corners. A loud clunk made the door shudder and it swung open by its own accord.

Thorn surmised that the door was constructed to keep people outside, since all of its moving parts were clearly visible from the inside. Poking his head through the opening, Thorn found the door opened to a little alcove close to the temple's mismatched roof. The outside of the hidden door looked like solid granite except for a small combination lock to one side. Five rotating wheels with over one hundred strange glyphs took place of a traditional door handle. Cracking the lock would be near impossible to anyone lucky enough to stumble on the hidden alcove but with the inner mechanisms visible to him, Thorn felt quite confident. Closing the door, Thorn remained inside the treasure room. He reached his small hands into the complex lock, spinning the unmarked wheels to puzzle out its combination. Several small notches marked the rotating wheels inside and it did not take long for Thorn to understand their purpose. Testing his assumptions with pressure and a wrist jiggle, one by one the tumblers and gears inside held. The fifth and final wheel turned into place with a satisfying click, causing the door to burst into motion once again.

Snatching his hand out as if burnt, the gears barely missed his fingers as they twisted in their mechanical dance. Once again the door swung open under its own power. This time, Thorn moved completely through the door, only now realizing the sun was setting. Inscribing the door's combination on the inside of his satchel with a piece of charcoal, Thorn spun the wheel locks randomly and closed the door. Something about the symbols on the lock seemed familiar to him, as if he had seen them in a dream, but Thorn was far too tired and sore to ponder. His main concern was sleep and medical attention. Translations and further exploration would come later. Satisfied with himself for the first time in years, Thorn moved from the hidden alcove, memorizing its location for future use. Unwinding a rope, he began his slow and painful descent, quietly dreading the march back to his bed.

The Lecture

"Peace is in single action and single thought. The wind blows and the trees move in unison, as should we," yet another irritating quote from Bromeliad, the local and wise soothsayer of the Tsanie Village.

Thorn's antisocial behavior and frequent expeditions to forbidden zones had earned him many of these lectures. The pompous fool just enjoyed the sound of his own voice, as if it were a privilege. To Thorn, he sounded akin to a buzzing gnat stuck in honey.

"The scrolls must be read to find inner peace and none will share their love if you continue to rebel. Unison in action and unison in thought, Thorn, for how are we expected to continue the peace if the peace is not present in... Thorn! Look at me when I'm speaking to you!"

Thorn had allowed his mind to wander yet again, wondering if ignoring the annoying voice would make it go away. The journey back from the temple had taken twice as long as expected and required four times the effort. This was thanks largely to his knee, swollen so large he would have to cut his trousers to get them off. The seemingly unending trek had sapped all energy from his body. In fact, the only reason Thorn was still awake had nothing to do with his willpower and everything to do with his discomfort. The itching cuts covering his body were now screaming at him with the same line in increasing volume.

Itch me. Itch me. Itch Me! ITCH ME!!!

If not for these persistent reminders, Thorn would have gone to sleep beneath a random tree hours ago. Glancing in Bromeliad's direction, it was clear the self-important ass needed some sort of verbal recognition to stop his prattling.

Mustering his most earnest expression, Thorn apologized.

"Bromeliad, my friend, there is nothing I would like more than to gallivant around naked whilst you read verses from the scrolls of foresight. I know many have gathered for the event and my perfect backside will be missed. But alas, I took a rather nasty tumble today and it ended with that beloved backside in a bramble patch, from quite a height mind you. Tonight's events, your droning voice and white asses in the moonlight just won't 'do it' for me. I'm sure you understand."

Patting Bromeliad on the shoulder, Thorn limped past him and headed towards the marketplace. He did not see the expression that marked Bromeliad's face, but as he walked a continuous stream of yelling poured out of the disgruntled soothsayer. Thorn allowed himself a small half grin before turning his attention to the herb shop, hoping that it would still be open this late. His knee would need some potent herbs to repair the damage of continued use.

"And you wonder why everyone avoids talking to you," a familiar voice attempting to sound deep came from behind a nearby tree.

"See that's where you are wrong Milia, people avoid me because of the company I keep. You know, the sort of shady characters that hide behind trees and talk in funny voices," said Thorn.

Stepping out from her hiding place, the sour-faced Milia responded, "It isn't a funny voice. It's ominous and scary. How did you know it was me?"

"As you just said, everyone avoids me, so who else could it be but you," explained Thorn.

Milia's expression of hurt feelings and slight confusion quickly turned to one of concern and she rushed to Thorn's side.

"Oh but look at you, you're hurt again. Your curiosity will be the end of you. Were you headed to the herbalists? I think it is pretty obvious that you were. Well now that I'm here, you need to go straight home to bed, because bed will give you rest and rest will help the healing. That's the last I will hear of it."

Finished with her quick verbal assault, Milia dashed in the herbalist's direction. In her wake, Thorn was left with a new challenge—making it home without collapsing from exhaustion.

The rest of the walk went by in a daze. Distance and time blurred and Thorn found himself focusing on the ground, willing his body to continue moving forward. It could have been half the night or just a short time later when Thorn's hands gripped the first rungs of his rope ladder. Hand over hand, with eyes closed, he made it to the top with muscles shaking from exertion. A falling sensation was accompanied by the satisfying image of a pillow rushing towards his face. Sleep had taken hold before he landed on his bedroll.

A short while later, the rosy cheeked Milia arrived, breathing heavily from the climb. Across her back she carried a sling full of assorted balms and ointments. Entering the hut quietly, she found Thorn face down and spreadeagled, snoring like an old grumpy bear. She moved to his side, placing down her goods, and began sorting them for use. Giving a snort of laughter and shaking her head in disbelief, she removed the shredded remains of Thorn's rabbit skin satchel before placing it on his bedside table.

Removing his clothing was not unlike peeling an onion. Trousers, tunic and boots had become fused to his body with a mixture of blood and grime. Settling in for the task at hand, Milia smiled and shook her head again thinking of how many times she had patched her friend up. No matter how injured Thorn got, he was never discouraged and continued to throw himself in harm's way. She admired his focus and determination, but above all else she loved his stories.

After his expeditions, Thorn really came alive. He would regale her with excited tales of treasures, traps and monstrous animals that never came close to the village. Milia was too afraid to go the places that Thorn did, but she was slowly building up her courage and would soon ask to join him. She didn't mind if the other Viridio shunned her like they did Thorn, adventure was worth the risk and he would protect her, she knew. Taking a deep breath, Milia started the long process of healing Thorn's broken body, a task that continued to the early hours of morning.

The Silver Sword

Dodging to the left, then to the right, the barbarian's axe swung low, biting into an unlucky bed post. Seizing the grip of Argath tightly, the blade sung beautifully as it cleared its scabbard. Three quick slices dismembered the important parts of a barbarian stupid enough to attack a Knight General in his home. These bastards would pay for their insolence. Three severed pieces of barbarian fell to the floor with a wet slap, but Knight General Patterson was already out of the room before they hit. Outside, he caught a screaming marauder by the back of his collar, wrenching him toward the waiting tip of Argath. The blade impaled with deadly efficiency. Kicking the fresh carcass off of his sword and down the stairs, the Knight General let out a guttural roar at the small horde *of barbarians chasing a little girl. Distracted, they turned to face him. Expressions of amusement morphed to confusion then finally to rage.*

Before their feeble minds could comprehend danger, Patterson launched into the air, bringing Argath's fury down upon a barbarian skull. Splitting the savage to his chest, the Knight General wrenched Argath out and thrust the blade through another neck. Finally recognizing the present danger, the barbarians let their fear show. Clumsy and unrefined swordplay demonstrated their lack of resolve, wildly swinging in aggressive arcs, both barbarians charged at once, stumbling into each other. The Knight General would usually toy with such pathetic individuals, but time was of the essence. Parrying two advances, he swiftly gripped the aggressor's sword arm and impaled him through the heart. Sliding Argath out of the barbarian's chest, the Knight General flicked an oncoming blade to the side, turning the last unlucky fool away, exposing his back. One fluid motion sliced through the top of his spine, and the man collapsed to the ground.

Watching for more threats, the Knight General sprinted in the direction of Swooping Hawk Gate. Any combatants in his path received swift and clean justice. Arriving in record time, the Knight General had amassed a half battalion of men that had been randomly scattered throughout the city.

Swooping Hawk Gate was breached when they arrived. Fallen defenders in their feather plate armor lay dead and dying as a stream of barbarians, confident and slow in their victory, trickled through the breach. Charging, Patterson's men stanched the flow of attackers quickly, reclaiming the gate. The invaders' ram had decimated the sturdy gate with surprising ease, punching a man-sized hole in the thick oaken wood. Whilst his men formed ranks, the Knight General faced the open plains beyond the gate. Banners of the invading forces flicked in a strong breeze outside the city wall. Silver Dragons, Golden Lotus, Runja's Circle—these were the banners of the Eastern Empire. At the forefront, however, men bore tall pine crosses with severed hands nailed to the wood.

"The Gworlug Tribe spearheaded the gate assault," Patterson said to himself, "but when did they start hiring themselves out to their enemies?"

Questioning the nearest guard, the latest reports confirmed the King and royal family were on the escape route but would need more time. Circling Vulture Gate and Raven's Claw Gate, both had fallen and the eastern forces had begun their advance. Nothing could be achieved by holding one gate if others fell. They would best serve now as a ploy for time—they must draw the enemy's attention. Knight General Patterson turned to his men and shouted.

"Gentlemen, it has been an honor to fight beside you and a pleasure to live with you. The King has asked for more time, and more time we shall give him! The masters of the sky shall feast well tonight and our souls will ride with them to redemption. Every foe you give them shall bring you favor. To our last breath we shall impede them. With every swing of our swords we shall hinder them further. You are the fighting men of Avion! Fulfill your Oath, Die With Honor!"

Charging the lines of Gworlug, Knight General Patterson led the attack. Slashing and stabbing, his blade Argath became a blur of white steel and red blood. Not every cut was fatal, but Argath was not picky in its blood lust. Holding the line, his men would only hinder the attackers, but the Knight General would have a death worthy of remembrance.

Focusing on the dark banners in the distance, he butchered his way to the fortified center of the invading forces. Death was everywhere and time passed swiftly, measured in corpses that fell to the gravel below like sand through an hourglass. The war fevered Knight General suddenly found himself before a monster of a man surrounded by heavily armored soldiers.

"Take that One," came the giant man's order.

Three men died in as many heartbeats as the Knight General lashed out in his final stand. The armored men ignored the danger, overwhelming with numbers. They hogtied Patterson with a crudely made rope. Twisting his neck from where he lay, face down on the gravel, he could see the ranks of barbarians part to let the enormous man through. This man obviously held authority, painted from head to toe in what appeared to be blood, his garb consisted of human skulls and bones collected from fallen enemies. The bones draped over his chain mail like a loose-fitting cloak, adding to the enormous space he already occupied.

"You need to give up this terrible charade. Do you think you can survive this? I plan to gut all the generals of your stupid nation," drool slathered the Chieftain's large, disproportionate chin as he spoke.

"I swear, you insolent swine, take one movement towards me and you shall lose something you hold most dear," threatened Patterson.

The Chieftain chuckled, deep and guttural. What possible threat could this lone warrior possess? He was bound at every limb and face down in the dirt, the threats had no foundation.

Leaning forward, the Chieftain's reeking breath wafted over his bound captive. Inches from Patterson's face the smell provided the most vicious assault of the day.

"Go... ahead."

Ripping the bonds apart from the sharpened rocks behind him, the Knight General struck the Chieftain in the face. Grabbing a rough stone in the confusion, Knight General Patterson smashed it directly into the gaping mouth of the formerly smug Chieftain. Reaching up Patterson gripped the back of the man's neck and struck twice more. As the barbarian yanked back from the onslaught the Knight General clung on tight using the motion to gain his feet. Broken teeth cascaded into the air, showering nearby barbarians with ivory splinters. Another strike crushed the Chieftain's big nose like an overripe tomato. Pain exploded across the Knight

General's flesh as spearheads tore through boiled leather and chain mail.

In the madness of death, a fit of laughter seized Patterson and he gripped the Chieftain close and whispered to him. "I have taken your face."

Releasing his grip, Patterson fell to the ground, landing on his knees. His defiant laughter rang through the quieted battlefield, broken only by the call of ravens approaching the feast, even as the Chieftain's curved blade swung towards his head.

Flailing around wildly, Thorn awoke screaming in agony as the spears impaled him over and over. The image of the curved sword coming closer made him instinctively roll sideways. Slamming into his bedside table, the movement caused the contents of his satchel to go scattering across the floor. The water skin containing the strange silver temple dust hit the floor just as the night table toppled, landing directly on top of it. The cork violently ejected and silver dust erupted across the floor. Still disoriented, Thorn barely noticed the brief flash of light that illuminated his room. Catching his breath, a calming wave of clarity washed over him as familiar surroundings filled his vision. Focusing on his breathing, Thorn attempted to lower his heart rate and clear his mind but it was proving more difficult than usual. He could still feel the spears stabbing deep, rendering his limbs useless. Looking down, Thorn realized the stiffness in his limbs came from the tight bandages that covered most of his body and the stabbing sensation was fading as he moved further from sleep. Turning his body into a sitting position, Thorn collapsed his head in his hands.

The nightmare had seemed so real, never before had he been able to ascertain that level of detail from the images that plagued him. Names, faces, troop movements and tactics, even the origins of sword and armor design were all milling around in Thorn's mind. After a few moments, he collected his thoughts and opened his eyes to survey the room. There were open containers of ointment lining the side of his bed and his toppled desk had sent many items flying around his hut. Off to one side a slight silver glow caught Thorn's eye. Unlike a candle's flickering light, this glow was constant and unchanging—like moonlight. Its origin appeared to be hidden behind his toppled bedside table. Standing up slowly and placing only slight pressure on his bad knee, Thorn hobbled over to the fallen table, peering over its edge.

Creasing his brow in confusion, Thorn found himself looking at an exact copy of the wicked curved sword that ended his haunted dream. Almost the same length as Thorn's bed, the sword looked exactly like something that would come out of a nightmare. The blade was coal-black and bowed outwards like the claw of a terrible beast. A strange and aggressive language was etched into the face of the blade, marking doom to those unlucky enough to see them. Everything about it screamed sharp pain from the spikes lining its spine down to the jagged grip and hilt which looked as dangerous as the blade's tip. How had this nightmare blade manifested? What was it doing here and what was to be done with it? These questions and more flooded Thorn's mind.

Moving in closer Thorn noticed that the blade may be blacker than night but somehow it exuded a slight glow. The sword from his dream had not done this. If anything the dream sword had swallowed light. Something was oddly familiar about the glow surrounding the sword. It was as if Thorn had seen it before, but he couldn't place it. Shifting his weight to peer closer, a sharp pain shot up his leg and the pieces of the puzzle fit together in his mind.

Damaged knee from the Temple—Temple where the treasure was found. Treasure that was melted by strange blood to silver dust ritual!

The silver dust was where Thorn had seen that glow before. Keeping one eye on the sword, Thorn searched the room for the water skin but to his dismay couldn't find it amongst the mess on the floor. Probing through his now empty satchel, Thorn systematically searched the rest of his hut, throwing things to the left and right. Finally lifting the bedside table, the empty water skin revealed itself. Thorn's attention, however, immediately focused on the scorch marks in the wooden floor previously hidden from his view. The thin smoldering gauges led in a line from the water skin's mouth directly to the hilt of the sword as if it had leapt out. There was no denying it to Thorn. The silver dust collected in the temple somehow constructed the sword or brought it forth using magic. It was either that, or Milia had used some of the fun mushrooms in her healing salves. If this was the case, Thorn would soon have a visit from the angry pink elephant that always expressed a need for pie.

Whatever the explanation was for the appearance of this foreign weapon, Thorn would treat it with the caution it deserved. Gingerly gripping the sword at its hilt, Thorn was able to half drag, half lift it over to lean on his bed. Grunting in annoyance, he saw that even when dragged sideways the sword left a nasty gash in his polished wooden floor. Feeling the full scope of his injuries, Thorn wrestled with the crude hunk of metal, making slow progress towards one wall. Leaning the blade upright, Thorn's focus was broken by a loud trumpeting from outside. The second sounding horn was a bugling whine signaling the day's second quarter. If Thorn didn't appear for his chores soon, someone would come looking for him. If they did that, they may find the sword. That would not end well.

Lowering the sword to the ground, Thorn searched for anything to mask the enormous glowing fang. He opted to move his comparatively lighter bed over the blade for safekeeping. Packing blankets and pillows around it for further concealment, Thorn was confident no one would stumble on it by accident. Reluctantly leaving his hut, Thorn slowly made his way to the day's chores, looking forward to his opportunity to study the sword closer and maybe even try it out.

Last Dance

Over the next painstaking week, Thorn was on his best behavior. He did not go so far as being nice to his neighbors, but tried to remain unobtrusive and bland. Any questions on how he received his quite severe injuries usually required little more than a change of subject to something more appealing.

Statements like, "how great is knuckle pea soup" and "I heard the western blueberries are riper than last year," would distract any nosy Viridio long enough for Thorn to depart.

However, it required all of his restraint not to verbally lash out at many of the Viridio for being their reliably stupid selves. On top of the constant pain from unhealed wounds, the burning desire to research the sword frustrated him. Many tests could not be achieved in his injured state and without Milia's intervention, his temper would have gotten the better of him several times. Lack of sleep was yet another obstacle to overcome. Since his successful expedition into the temple's treasure room, every single night held new and more terrifying nightmares. Sometimes he was a barbarian, other times a soldier in a mighty battle. He even faced mighty and terrible beasts as a combatant in a vast underground chamber. Hordes of spectators cheered him on, even as the horned beasts tore at his entrails. The variety and venue changed, but every scene ended the same way. Watching through these people's eyes, Thorn died over and over in new horrific and violent ways. The pain of his inevitable demise awoke him to the chorus of his own screams that now came unbidden.

Towards the end of the week, Thorn's knee was reacting positively to

Milia's treatments. The pain had receded, hopefully the stiffness would soon follow suit. Unfortunately it seemed one discomfort dissipated as a new one surfaced. Troubling events had correlated closely with the increase of his nightmares. The forest had always been still and silent within Tsanie Village as it was in many forbidden zones Thorn had visited. In other parts of the forest, animals would hunt and kill whatever they pleased. The night brought the most dangers. Within the village, however, all creatures large and small would feel a sense of security, ceasing nocturnal activity to slumber with the Viridio.

It was a subtle change, but new animals, birds and reptiles had begun to fill the silence with their voice in the depth of night. Creatures that did not belong seemed to be congregating at the invisible boundaries that surrounded Tsanie. They seemed agitated, as if they sensed danger and wanted sanctuary. Something seemed to be changing within the forest and it gave Thorn an uneasy feeling. He knew something needed to be done, but in his sleep deprived state the answer eluded him. So the animal's odd behavior was buried in his mind as tired paranoia.

The new moon rose next to the sun, signaling that the day of Rest and Ritual was upon the village yet again. As the two celestial brothers held hands to walk the sky together, the Viridio would celebrate in the only way they thought appropriate. Donning nothing but bare skin, the children would spend the entire day resting to watch the brothers walk. When the moonless sky darkened, most of the night would be spent dancing around campfires whilst ritualistic psalms were sung. The reason for the naked fool's energetic display was to satisfy the natural urges that came from being children of the nymphs. Thorn had never felt these urges so to him it was a great waste of time.

The day passed quickly with no one disturbing him as he expected, but as the sun's glow waned through the canopy there was a heavy knock on his door.

"Happy Passing's Day, Thorn!" came Milia's cheerful voice.

Thorn let out a condescending snort, which was interpreted as *'come on in Milia and share in my happiness.'* Letting herself in, Milia performed a quick pirouette and landed on Thorn's bed, bouncing him a little.

"So how are we feeling today?" she questioned.

Thorn stared at her with tired itchy eyes. The dark bags beneath them resembled blueberry stains and his face felt greasy despite bathing just the day before.

"I guess that's a bit of a rhetorical question, considering your predicament," said Milia.

Continuing his stare, Thorn creased his eyebrows to her matter-of-fact statement. Opening his mouth to inhale, he began to speak only to be immediately interrupted.

"Don't look at me like that! You know what I'm talking about," said Milia, poking him with an accusing finger. "Bromeliad has said time and time again it is not healthy for us to miss the ritual dances. Yet time and time again you miss them and always end up in some sort of pain. I remember the last time I asked you to dance and you disappeared. Two days later you came back limping with no trousers and burn marks. Where the pants went, I don't know, but your urges clearly take you to dangerous places."

Thorn had learnt not to argue with Milia when it came to dancing. It wasn't the traditions that she cared for, but rather the dancing itself. She had been gifted with the ability to move and twist as smoothly as a leaf caught in a gentle breeze. Even Thorn enjoyed watching her dance. It was actually her skilled dancing that drew his interest at the start of their friendship.

"I guess that's why your life is so fulfilled and lacking in urges. I have seen you dancing in the kitchen, the bathroom, the store, the..." Cutting Thorn off, Milia nodded her head in agreement.

"I know you're being sarcastic, but have you any other reason for me being so fantastic? Hmmmmmm?" Her lip pouted forward in mock defiance. "Our mothers are beautiful and want us to dance beautifully for them. Even you can be beautiful if you want to."

"Well, come to think of it just the other day I had my clothes ripped off by a giant Milikak beetle when I was trying to collect its honey," Thorn responded. "As I ran stark naked through the trees, I did dance a little to taunt it. Really was quite liberating."

"Then I expect to see you tonight in all of your beetle taunting glory," said Milia, smiling. "Just remember... Bromeliad has a shorter temper than most Milikak beetles *and* knows where you live."

Happily patting Thorn on the head like an infant, Milia stood and pirouetted out of the room spinning the opposite direction as when she had entered. A few seconds passed before her head darted back into the doorway.

"Thorn! Strip, smile, dance. Let's go."

Accepting that fatigue would render any of his arguments halfhearted and useless, Thorn gave in and prepared for the night's festivities. After all, he did owe Milia and it was partially his fault she was so headstrong. Her assistance and knowledge of herb craft had shaved months off of his healing time. Soon he would be well enough to venture back to the Temple for more exploration.

Stripping down, Thorn cursed his still painfully stiff joints. Inspecting the bandage on his knee, Thorn concluded it would not need replacing, which was a relief. The sun and moon had disappeared behind the tree line and Milia was growing impatient. Finishing his preparations, they began their descent from the great tree together. Thorn walked casually, whilst Milia danced and twirled around him, full of energy and excitement. Making their way towards the Meadow of Glee, they could hear the sounds of drums beating a quick cheerful rhythm and flutes tweeting in chorus. The music grew louder as they approached.

Small fires spotted the meadow, throwing giant shadows of movement on the nearby trees. Hundreds of long-handled torches were driven into the ground, lighting even the darkest patches of the large meadow. In the absence of moonlight, everything outside of the well-lit meadow seemed nonexistent. The Viridio children were circling an enormous tree stump in the meadow's center, cartwheeling and dancing about like a big naked whirlpool. Their funneling movement drew the eye to the center stump on which an assortment of musicians sat. Hands beat drums in a furious rhythm for the harps and flutes to follow. Chanting could be heard over the lively tune in an eerie chorus. Standing dead center on a raised platform, three sages held their hands high, speaking the ancient words. One of the three preached louder than the others with his familiar droning voice. Bromeliad's little potbelly was shining in the firelight like a white river rock deprived of sun. It reflected the light like polished metal, making him a fat little beacon on his pedestal.

The excitement on Milia's face was palpable. She fidgeted and bopped around, barely able to restrain herself, but clearly didn't want to leave Thorn's side. Just like an excited puppy, her head turned from the festivities to Thorn then back again, as if waiting for the command to run off and join the fun.

"Go on," Thorn gave a half-tilted nod in the meadow's direction. "I promise I'll join you shortly."

There was no sun or moon, but Milia's smile could have replaced them both and lit the night sky, it was so bright. She was off in a flash, jumping and somersaulting towards the fray of dancing Viridio children. Milia soon disappeared into the swarm of massing bodies.

Thorn stood watching the display for quite awhile, but after receiving several sour looks, he finally buckled and joined the dancers. Now close to the central stump, Bromeliad's voice could definitely be heard booming over the music. He read the verses that had been passed down for as long as anyone could remember. Time passed slowly as the music lulled and raised in tempo. The dances changed in a seamlessly fluid motion from tumbling spins to gentle twirls. Several times Thorn found Milia in the fray, twisting and turning with unparalleled grace. Her mirthful smile betrayed her smug satisfaction for pressuring Thorn to join the dances. Seeing her expression of victory made Thorn surprisingly competitive. Although he tried to keep up with her, she moved through the crowd with a speedy grace and he was soon left behind.

The night progressed and the fires burnt low but still the Viridio danced. Upon completing an impressive sideways flip, a flicker of light deep in the trees caught Thorn's eye. Stopping abruptly, two Viridio bumped into his back, knocking Thorn off balance. He stood and quickly shoved them away, keeping his eyes fixed on the flicker in the distance. One Viridio went tumbling into another group, causing a pileup, whilst the other hit the center stump face first, leaving a bloody mark. The silence was deafening as the music abruptly stopped. All eyes were fixed on Thorn, watching with shocked and appalled expressions.

Something is wrong, thought Thorn. *The light in the trees is not natural and it's moving towards the meadow.* Transfixed, Thorn ignored the faces of onlookers and slowly climbed onto the large tree stump for a better vantage point. Bromeliad was yelling curses at him in quick succession until Thorn's clasping hand covered the Soothsayer's mouth. Peculiar actions mixed with Thorn's steady stare began to cause confusion within the Viridio and as his gaze intensified, others turned to follow his stare. Their unnaturally blue eyes pierced the darkness of the forest in unison.

"What is that...?" a younger Viridio to the right of Thorn whispered.

His lips had barely formed the last word, when giant silhouetted monsters burst from the tree line. The creatures skittered on all fours with bellies close to the ground and sharp whipping tails. They looked like giant lizards with oddly long snouts and dark mahogany scales. Splashes of fluorescent yellows and blues cut across the dark scales, providing a robust contrast with the green forest surroundings. As they moved further into the clearing, Thorn could make out men covered in black spikes riding the huge reptiles. Their faces were painted the same colors as their creatures and many held bundled nets and long spears.

The Viridio stood awestruck, Thorn among them. A cold chill rolled down his spine and a feeling of dread tightened in the pit of his stomach. Frozen as if in ice, Thorn struggled to comprehend the image unfolding in front of him. Behind the stunned silence a voice within his head hissed.

"RUN!"

Jolting into action Thorn vaulted off of the stump and hit the ground running. Desperately searching for Milia, he moved to the edge of the crowd, the voice repeating itself with more urgency now.

"RUN! RUN! RUN!"

Shoving past motionless Viridio, the voice almost shouted.

"THE SWORD!"

Ignoring the pain in his leg, Thorn focused on his new goal. A spinning whistling sound rose in the distance, quickly moving closer. A shout to Thorn's left drew his attention as a Viridio collapsed, his legs wrapped in a tar-covered rope. The men on the lizards were amongst the Viridio now, causing mayhem. Some held long nets between riders, scooping up a group of Viridio before dumping them to the ground like netted fish. Others were spinning rope above their heads, throwing it at individuals that ran for the village. Viridio children were falling over left and right like freshly cut saplings in a winter storm. Thorn rolled to the left, narrowly avoiding a spinning rope as it clacked to the ground. Gripping it in one hand Thorn used its weighted ends to build up momentum then tossed it at a nearby rider. The spinning projectile missed its target by a wide margin, but by some queer luck it struck a lizard monster in the side of the head. Clawing at its eye the lizard monster bucked it rider to the ground, only to trample him moments later.

Ignoring the cries of the flattened man, Thorn continued his fast pace until he finally hit the tree line. Trees whizzed by, causing the terrified screams of the Viridio to echo strangely down quiet paths. Animal screeches mixed with angry shouts, then a loud 'bang,' shocked Thorn's legs to move even faster. He tried to ignore the noise and forge on, but his fear of the unknown made him jump at any new sound. He could not save them, not yet. He needed a weapon, a big one.

Darting past the market square, Thorn slammed into his rope ladder. Gripping it tight, he scrambled up faster than ever before. Reaching the top without a moment's pause, Thorn threw his bed to one side, gripping the monster blade that hid below. In his haste, he had forgotten the sword's immense weight, but before logic pierced his terror-clouded mind, the blade was off of the floor and heading for the exit. Some strange magic coursed through Thorn's veins, rendering the sword as light as a feather. Running outside, he hurled the sword into the air before him. It spun, suspended on nothing for one impossible moment, then arced downward through the dark toward the riverbank below. Following suit, Thorn took a deep breath then launched himself towards the waiting river, hoping it was not too late.

Adrenalin coursed through his veins and the fall seemed slower than usual. Taking in his surroundings as he fell, Thorn could see the evil men had followed him through the trees. Lizard riders now roamed the Tsanie walkways with burning torches. Men on foot spread out in the market square like angry fire ants. *Fall faster damn it,* thought Thorn.

Hitting the water hard, he quickly pushed himself to the surface, leaving foam and bubbles in his wake. Out of the darkest depths, Thorn streamed towards the riverbank underwater and hidden from view. He slithered onto the riverbank, quietly watching for any of the intruders. Only gently moving water and darkness met his searching eyes until a familiar glow caught his attention.

The sword had hit the dirt, tip first, until only its grip was visible. The impact had driven the rest of the enormous weapon below the soil. Ripping it out of the ground, Thorn quickly dove behind a tree just as the fiery light of a torch appeared. A gurgling click, almost like a wet growl, accompanied the torch-bearing man as he moved past. Thorn indulged the idea of killing the man and his noisy creature, but he needed to be smart. Stealth was the only advantage he had at the moment and it could only be used once.

Defiance

Sneaking through the trees and staying out of sight, he made his way towards the Meadow of Glee. Milia had to be saved so both of them could escape the men's evil intentions. Thorn focused on gaining height as he advanced toward the meadow. By the time he reached the edge of the tree line he was on a high catwalk with a superb field of view. Squatting low, he skulked in the shadows, observing the unfolding events. The mounted men that had come through the trees first were just the beginnings of a much larger force. There were now more than fifty men in the clearing with even more pouring through the trees. Others moved through Tsanie Village, searching for stragglers. The ones on foot were herding the Viridio children into a large group towards the center of the meadow prodding, and hitting them with their spears. Excluding himself, it looked as if not a single Viridio had escaped the Meadow of Glee when it was attacked. Since festival attendance was compulsory most of the village was captured in one foul swoop. At a cursory glance, Thorn estimated over ninety percent of the village was now held prisoner in the meadow.

The first waves of men had been very thorough in their hunt and were clearly professionals. Their weapons were designed to hinder and detain rather than kill. The added speed and shock value of their monstrous lizards increased their already clear advantage. The Viridio didn't stand a chance. As Thorn watched, the circle of marauders cleared a path and a tall skinny man made his way towards the huddled captives. The man was dressed neck to toe in solid black leathers, a silhouette in the already dark meadow. He spoke to the group as he paced back and forward, moving his hands to accentuate his demands. Thorn strained to hear his words but his voice blended with the general night noise and was rendered inaudible. Whatever was said clearly terrified the Viridio as their already scared faces contorted with new levels of fear. Some began to cry and sob whilst others shook their heads in denial.

The leader continued his distressing monologue until one of the children stood to interrupt loud enough that the words carried even to Thorn. It was Milia, and she was yelling so hard her face was turning red. A stream of profanities, the likes of which Thorn had never heard, spewed from her angry little mouth. Thorn smiled inwardly, enjoying her defiance in the face of these dangerous men whom she had just referred to as 'bastard sons of pig mongrels'. His smile was almost immediately erased as the leader moved toward the shouting girl with long quick strides. A loud crack replaced her profanity as the back of the tall man's hand whipped across Milia's face, spraying blood into the air. Her limp body hit the ground, flopping like a dead fish.

Thorn's breathing quickened and his heart pounded swiftly in his ears. White knuckles tightened on the sword's grip as he trembled with rage. Anger rose in Thorn then like never before. Spots clouded his vision and he watched with gritted teeth as the skinny man placed his foot firmly on Milia's throat. Pushing down, he forced a gurgled yelp from her as she scrambled pathetically for freedom. With surprise, Thorn realized he was no longer stationary. He had burst out of cover, dropped to the forest floor and was sprinting towards the closest lizard rider. As if possessed, he let out a blood-curdling scream and leapt at the intruder, swinging the sword in a horizontal arc. Two equal pieces of man hit the grass with a wet thud. Slamming his foot on the saddle of the beast, Thorn launched himself at yet another enemy, this time impaling him and riding his body to the meadow floor. Dodging the snapping maws of several beasts, Thorn rolled to his feet, charging headfirst at the leader.

Two marauders were fast enough and reacted to Thorn's surprise attack. They engaged his charge with weapons raised in defense. Slapping the first spear thrust to the side with the flat of his blade, Thorn didn't miss a step. His momentum and the blade's weight opened the first man's throat. The second attacker moved his sword in anticipation, trying to block Thorn's slow hulking swing. The blades collided with a jarring effect, throwing the man backwards with unexpected power. The smaller weapon snapped from the stress, following its owner awkwardly to the ground. A quick downward thrust impaled the man, finishing his resistance.

Ignoring the spray of red mist hitting his face, Thorn sprang high into the air, continuing his assault. The sword arced in an overhead slice towards the leader's face but before hitting its mark, a heavy studded boot heel slammed into Thorn's chest. The thin man had spun and delivered a kick, stopping him dead in the air. Collapsing in a broken heap to the ground, Thorn gasped for air like a beached fish but his lungs refused to obey. Through blurred vision, he searched in vain for the sword that was no longer in his hand.

Arm over arm, Thorn crawled as fast as he could towards the shimmering metal in the grass a few yards away. He was abruptly stopped when pressure crushed down between his shoulder blades, pinning him to the ground. For a moment, Thorn struggled helpless, like an upturned tortoise, but it was no use. He could not get away. In his oxygen-deprived mind, no better solutions presented themselves, so Thorn just focused on breathing. The pressure disappeared for one glorious moment of air before it was replaced with pain. A steel-studded boot shattered Thorn's rib cage, crashing into his side. Stunned from the strike and unable to move, the boot continued its bludgeoning with three more kicks. Every punt became harder, with the third sending him spinning across the grass in a tumbling mess.

Staring skyward at the glimmering stars, his lungs still refused to cooperate. Through dulling vision, the splendor of the night's sky regressed to a smudged spotty mess. This smear of light was then eclipsed by a slender silhouette towering above. The silhouette lifted its leg and brought down a large boot. It landed on Thorn's chest, squeezing what little air remained out in a wet wheeze. The leader was speaking to him, but through the ringing in Thorn's ears he could only make out the words 'protector' and 'cute.' A chorus of laughter erupted into the night as the men enjoyed the victory. Leaning down, the man increased the pressure on Thorn's chest, bringing his face closer. Blinking back tears, Thorn felt like he was drowning in open air. No matter how hard he tried, he couldn't make out the features of the man's face except his manic grin, shining madly in the torchlight.

"I don't give two shits about my men, but their lives are not yours to take. They are mine. I will need a few lives from you to rectify this," he said. The dark-clad man looked up from Thorn, eyes scanning the huddled captives. "I think the mouthy girl you attempted to save would be a good start."

The sinister grin evaporated as he removed his boot from Thorn's chest and moved out of vision. Fear blew the fog from Thorn's addled mind, replaced quickly by the burning rage that prompted his initial assault. Turning over slowly, Thorn rose to one knee and launched into a new attack. Taking two steps, he threw himself at the man's back. There was a blur of motion and in midair the tackle was stopped by a punch to Thorn's chest, harder than anything he had ever experienced. His arms dropped limply and his knees buckled but somehow he remained upright, swaying, and stared into the skinny man's face. The man's expression had changed to one of angry disappointment.

"What a waste. You could have served him so well," he said, sadly.

Confused, Thorn realized the thin man was holding the sword Thorn had just dropped. Thorn's eyes followed the blade from the hilt to where the tip ended in his chest. Sparks tingled down his spine, radiating pain, as his own blood decorated the blade in a red spray. Thorn's eyes shifted out of focus, as if he had stared at the sun for too long and was now trying to see in a darkened room. As the darkness closed in, a cold sensation of vertigo washed over him. Tingling pinpricks wrapped Thorn's feet and hands, moving inwards, until they enveloped his entire body. An icy numbness followed.

Through glazed eyes, Thorn saw the sword glow white where his blood had painted it. The glow brightened for a split second, then with a flash the blade melted, sifting away like river sand. Without the sword's support, Thorn's limp body rocked forward, falling to the grass. He did not feel the impact, could not see the impact. The only thing in Thorn's world at that moment was the sound of a solitary high-pitched scream, but it too faded into the distance as the darkness overwhelmed his senses.

The Fall

The deafening roar was steadily increasing in volume and Thorn wasn't sure where he was anymore. Thorn, if that was even his name. He hadn't always been called that. Every time he gripped at memories, they would slip through the cracks in his mind. Just like a handful of snow, the images would slowly melt away until he held nothing. It was infuriating. The sword had definitely hit its mark, but what was that glowing and dissolving it had done just before everything had gone black. *What sword am I thinking of... do I own a sword?* Surely strange magic had intervened or this was the afterlife. Was he dead, or about to be born? Perhaps this was punishment for the gooseberries he had stolen last week or the melons the week before. Continuous falling through darkness seemed like a harsh punishment for a few food thefts. The rushing noise was increasing. He feared it would continue until he finally lost his sanity.

He had no sense of time during this perpetual descent. Without his senses, he was disoriented. Vision, smell, taste and touch were lost to him. Only the loudest of rushing noises and a deep lurching in his stomach accompanied this nothingness. The roars of distant waterfalls were coming to meet him. Thorn welcomed the crisp feeling of water as it always cleared his mind and started the day off right. Thinking was more difficult now, logic was non-existent. *Perhaps this is a dream; things don't need to make sense in a dream.* Connecting past experiences and current events seemed impossible with a bending twisting timeline. The puzzle pieces all fit together easily, but the completed picture was wrong. He remembered events clearly but they stitched together in impossible ways. Ever present, the deafening roar in the background was destroying any reserve of concentration Thorn possessed.

"Wake up!" He screamed in his mind, as if this were a dream. Reality reiterated the truth with jumbled memory. Milia was screaming and then...

"Death," whispered a voice, together familiar and strange.

It was a hard slap to the face. The truth dawned and memories sorted themselves, burning their way deep into Thorn's mind. Like waking from a dream after believing it was reality, Thorn felt like a fool. Pictures of the events lit his vision, moving faster and faster until they abruptly halted. Frozen was the last image his mortal eyes had seen. Like a highly detailed painting, the sneering face of a tall skinny man dressed in black was revealed in all of its gory detail. Seeing that image made something click and Thorn's eyes snapped open, as if for the first time.

In utter calm, Thorn tumbled head over heels towards an enormous ocean below with nothing but a pitch black sky above. Moving faster and faster he hurtled like a falling meteor, but there was no air rushing past his face. Trying desperately to slow his spin, his maneuvers lacked necessary air resistance and were too late. Slamming face first into the water, frothy bubbles filled his vision. Expecting a painful sting from the fall and a bone numbing cold from the angry ocean, Thorn was pleasantly surprised. The impact felt like a bag of feathers and the expected cold was instead a delicious warmth that hugged his body. All of his pains and confusion washed away. The bad dreams were distant memories that happened to someone else.

Relaxing completely, Thorn melted in the water. The sense of euphoria was intoxicating and, hopefully, never ending. His eyes rolled back whilst he took a deep breath. The water rushed into his nose resembling the smell of a thousand flowers on a summer day. Thorn could even feel the sun on his skin at that moment. Everything about this liquid was pleasure and relaxation. Floating in the current just below the surface, Thorn's limp body moved ever onward towards a final destination unknown to him. The ecstasy was interrupted when a voice in his head whispered

"Up"

Ignoring it once, the whisper came again.

"Up"

Without thinking Thorn opened his eyes a slit. Trying to appease the whispering voice he pushed his body upwards with a single stroke of his arms. Breaking the surface of the water with his face, Thorn immediately thrashed to dive away from the pain. His face was on fire, both freezing cold and burning hot at the same time. Instantly awake now, Thorn's skin was throbbing from the burns he had just received.

"UP!" commanded the whisper, urgent now.

Thorn shook his head in the water, clamping both hands over his ears. There was no way he was going above the water again, but as hard as he tried, the voice could not be ignored. Again and again the whisper repeated its message until finally the message changed.

"Up or she dies!"

A hazy image devoid of color forced its way into Thorn's mind. He was looking at a large room filled with pillows and silks. Towards the center, an enormous round bed supported the bulging form of a fat man dressed in flowing robes. He was shoveling meats into his mouth from a tray held by a small child collared like a dog. One hand ate whilst the other stroked the boy's arm in an overly familiar way. The fat man's eyes looked bloodshot and his movement betrayed heavy intoxication. The fat man's hand brushed the boy's neck causing him to flinch with disgust. The movement unbalanced the tray flipping greasy meats onto a nearby silk cushion.

Spitting a mouthful of half chewed sausage into the air, the fat man angrily backhanded the child. The boy hit the ground hard and then was lifted into the air by his collar. Back and forward the child shook as the man yelled obscenities in a strange language. In a moment, the child became as limp as a wet noodle. Lolling his head around, the fat man looked at the dead thing he now held with mild disappointment. He tossed it to one side, hitting a small gong with the lifeless corpse. Out of a side door came another child, this one was a girl with blonde hair. Lifting her head, she allowed the fat man to clip a new collar around her neck, then bowed and kissed both of his feet.

A new tray of food was offered to the man and Thorn suddenly realized the girl was Milia. Her face now showed none of the happiness or joy it had once exuded. A thin dark tattoo now marked her cheek. Like a drop of ink, it traced a dark line down her face and neck. She was pale and looked so different but it was definitely her.

"No... No... NO!" Thorn screamed.

The water clouded with bubbles with every silent denial. She needed to get away or he would kill and toss her aside like the previous child. The image faded, replaced by the calming warmth of the strange water. Somehow, after Thorn's vision the ocean seemed colder and less comforting. Struggling 'up' just as the voice commanded wasn't working. Every time Thorn broke the surface of the water, searing pain beyond imagination was there to meet him. The invisible fire licked at his skin until it forced his retreat. The burning made the water's numbing embrace ever more attractive every time he failed. Again, Thorn pushed his way out of the water and again, he was forced to retreat as the invisible fire scorched his flesh. A muted scream of agony bubbled its way out of Thorn's mouth as he gripped his face with both hands.

"Up Now!"

The whisper had a crackling sense of urgency to it this time. Something was obviously wrong. The image of Milia flooded his mind again and with one last push he thrust his torso through the water's surface. The inferno instantly blasted his skin, but fighting through the anguish, Thorn kicked his legs and held his body above the surface. Closing his eyes, he embraced the pain until it was too much, and he collapsed forward exhausted.

To his surprise, Thorn's chest hit solid ground and he scrambled to find a hand hold. Dragging the rest of his body out of the water was difficult. As he struggled, it felt like he was being flayed by the water's surface, leaving all of his skin behind. Finally, Thorn dragged his left leg out of the water and was rewarded with instant pain relief as the burning stopped. Sitting up, Thorn found himself on a small desert island as big as a barrel. He scanned his surroundings but there was nothing but water in all directions as far as the eye could see. The island that he had dragged himself onto appeared to have come from nowhere, apparently manifesting right when Thorn had needed it. It was constructed of strange clear sand that floated above the water and yet it was stable against the current surrounding it.

Letting out a sigh of relief, Thorn sat forward resting his arms on his knees.

Casually he peered over the edge of the island half expecting to see flayed remains similar to a snake that had shed its skin. The hair on the back of his neck stood erect and his muscles tensed. Staring back at him was a wide-eyed ghostly figure reaching from just below the water's surface. The ghost was Thorn, or at least a pale apparition that looked exactly like him. The terrified boy that had never escaped the confines of the water clawed and hammered its fists on the invisible wall between water and air. Frothy bubbles coursed from its mouth in fits of fearful rage, its angry eyes fixed on Thorn.

Suddenly the anger was gone and only fear marked its face. The clawing at the water's surface became frantic as the current slowly moved it away from the island. Longing eyes pleaded and begged whilst ghostly lips silently mouthed *'No'* over and over. Unable to fight the current, the water dragged the ghost away until Thorn could no longer make it out in the distance. Warm drops of liquid pattered onto Thorn's outstretched hands and he suddenly realized he was crying. Sure, watching himself or an image of himself in so much pain and fear was disturbing but why was he reacting like this. He suddenly felt hollow.

The Librarian

"What is this emptiness? Why do I feel like a part of me just died?" he asked out loud. From behind came a lecturing voice, responding to the question Thorn had just asked.

"Very astute, young one, for that is precisely the exhibition witnessed, a detachment or division of one's eternal soul in metamorphosis. The current being of single plane existence now awarded the multitude available. Or in layman's terms, giving up part of your soul for the chance of rebirth."

Thorn turned to look behind and found a straight-backed old man standing on the island. He squinted with a knowing look that suggested he had witnessed the whole event. The old man's eyes were slightly obscured behind the thick dusty spectacles perched on his long narrow nose. He wore an impressive dark gray doublet with a coal-black vest over the top. The vest was fastened with dark wooden clasps and a long leather belt. His trousers were of similar crisp material, providing an outfit that looked as sharp as his words had just been. His clean-shaven face betrayed no emotion as it regarded Thorn's tear-covered cheeks.

"Your expression appears perplexed and rightfully so, such confusion with no answers and questions in exponential growth," the spectacled man continued, "I would solicit you to inquire, but alas time is a fleeting and fickle beast and one which grows shorter with age. Regardless, your questions would be feeble-minded and apparent. Thus, I shall present you with concurrent facts. You are a Viridio Infinitatus, but unlike most, you are something of a rarity. Your father was an exceptionally important individual and for this reason alone my employer has taken keen interest in your expiration date. And so we are led to your existing predicament. You are indeed dead, but at the same time you are not. This is due to aforementioned vested interest in your expiry. Currently you reside on a makeshift island providing a picturesque panorama of the Necrononicanal, or sea of the dead. Your crossing was unpredictably brisker than originally anticipated, so kudos for that. Limbo can be such a nuisance to navigate at the best of times."

Pulling at a silver chain that loosely hung from a vest pocket, the man tugged until a circular device no bigger than a coin emerged. He raised it to his eyes, studied it for half a heartbeat then returned it to its home.

"As for your conceptual understanding of time, let us just say it lacks grounding. You will find, without a living body, time becomes a disjointed entity. There are no seasons in death. However, for someone who misplaces time, the line of questioning is predictably linear so let's progress in order. You have been dead for exactly 20 years 4 months and 27 days. With mortality and timeline addressed, it is only courteous to answer the question that has plagued you throughout my monologue by introducing myself. You may call me the Librarian as I arrange and categorize information. My purpose currently centers on your protection and transition to the next phase. Unfortunately, as previously stated, we lack time, a fact made blatantly obvious by the red mist converging from the east. It is indeed time to vacate."

Thorn turned in the direction the Librarian had indicated. Off on the horizon, a collection of dark red clouds billowed forward, moving swiftly toward the island. Twisting and churning on themselves, they appeared to be expanding in size like fast-growing mushrooms. Thorn's head was still reeling from the overload of information suddenly forced upon him as well as the difficulty it had taken to decipher. He wished the strange man would talk like a normal person. As the bloated red mass increased its speed, Thorn turned to the Librarian, opening his mouth in an attempt to voice his concerns. He was quickly cut off.

"Young one, you mustn't concern yourself with trivial matters beyond control, transportation is pending and my employer is never behind schedule," said the Librarian.

Whilst talking, the old man tilted his head up, searching for something far above. He slowly raised his arm until it was pointing directly at the sky. Thorn followed the Librarian's gaze, straining his eyes to see what the old man saw. Nothing but an empty darkness painted the roof of the world. Thorn opened his mouth again to question, when suddenly a black rope whipped down and wrapped its way around the librarian's arm. Steam hissed from where the living rope touched skin, filling the air with the scent of burning flesh. Thorn watched in horror, fixated on the writhing length and what it was doing to the Librarian's arm. Musing on the boy's obvious shock, the Librarian tilted his head slightly to the side. Faster than a striking snake, he was plucked up into the sky and disappeared from view.

Thorn gawked up in confusion, straining to find the Librarian. He couldn't make out anything in the dark sky. In the blink of an eye, another rope darted down from the gloom and hit Thorn. Unable to react to resist it, the wriggling thing wrapped its way around Thorn's neck and torso. Struggling feebly against its vice-like grip, Thorn winced, anticipating the burning pain that was sure to follow but nothing happened. The tentacle was clearly touching Thorn's skin yet there was no steam or burning. The contact just left a cool sensation, almost as if it were made of cold marble. Looking closer, Thorn saw it was not rope that constricted his chest but something more like a dry tentacle or creeping vine. The tendril was not solid black either; it had lightly colored runes and symbols marking their way back and forth along its surface. There was something oddly familiar about the symbols. He only glanced at them briefly before he too launched into the sky.

Feeling like a rag doll at the mercy of a giant child, Thorn hurtled into the air, barely able to move. At the tremendous speed, the force on his body made him feel like stone. Every limb was one hundred times heavier than before, but Thorn still managed to force his head skyward. Ahead, a small blot, somehow darker than the unchanging sky, grew bigger every second. As Thorn rushed towards it, he realized it was actually a tear in the sky, an enormous gaping wound with nothing but blackness without depth within. It appeared to drink the darkness of the surrounding sky like a hungry mouth. Knowing there was no use resisting his fate, Thorn relaxed his muscles and prepared himself for the next stage in his absurd afterlife.

The darkness instantly enveloped everything it touched. Thorn was no exception. He burst through the gap of space and time, finding emptiness within. The lack of depth and perception resembled the former limbo he had experienced, but there were subtle differences. For one, he was in his right mind, a feat that seemed impossible when floating through the darkness of limbo. The other change was an overwhelming sense of awe that sent Thorn's stomach into knots. He had only experienced a semblance of this feeling before, when staring into the eyes of a great jungle cat. The vast sense of unimportance crushed Thorn like a mountain. Anxiety and fear built to uncomfortable levels before a booming voice began to speak. It reverberated around the obscurity, shouted and whispered from a thousand different mouths.

"In the beginning there were five brothers, each with their claim to the power of the world. To fight and quarrel did not befit their station. The oldest of the brothers proposed a game of wits to ascertain the most worthy. The game required many pieces and would be played on a board like no other. As of yet no victor has been decided, but they will never see you coming. It is time to move onto the board, my child."

Every word resonated with power and by the end, Thorn's head throbbed painfully. Images then began whizzing through the darkness. Some moved faster than others, but as they passed Thorn was assaulted with visions of violence and death. Not all displayed pain, some were accompanied by flashes of warmth and happiness but the anger and fear of death was overwhelming. The more he witnessed, the closer their relationship became until Thorn could see ties between events, linking them together. The visions were increasing in speed and voices began chanting in unison.

"A man stands alone in pain and in doubt.
For the reaper has come to snuff his flame out
What once was within will now go without
As the windows are open and the soul doth fly out
Although you might think this gift to be a curse
If patience persists and if you coerce

Even when heaven or hell is in sight
My soul becomes yours before it takes flight"

The visions were blinding and the pain was unbearable. More voices joined the chanting now, faster and louder. Building intensity, the words decomposed, becoming a scrambled mess until soon the voices corroded entirely, replaced by an ear-piercing screech. Thorn thought he knew pain before, but he was wrong. The terrible sound vibrated his very soul whilst a searing heat burned from the inside out. The fire was so painfully intense he welcomed death.

"Kill Me! PLEASE!" Thorn screamed into the din.

Laughter rose through the mind-numbing pain and with a deafening crack of lightning the pain stopped. Raw tingling covered sensitive skin and with a gasp, air filled his unused lungs. Every breath was beautiful agony followed by harsh coughing. Just like a thirsty man in the desert, Thorn drank air greedily. Lightheaded and woozy, he opened his eyes. Plumes of steam cascaded off of his body, rising to the ancient stone ceiling above. The coughing fit slowly subsided, but his body continued to shake and twitch in uncontrollable ways. He had never felt so tired in his life.

Eyes still swimming with mist, Thorn could not see much except the dark marble bowl he found himself in. Struggling to sit up, his body shook from effort but as his head rose the room revealed itself. Mountains of gold and gems were piled close by and a statue regarded him with a half-melted face. Thorn was back in the temple. The spots in his vision danced, reducing the world to a pinhole as unconsciousness threatened. Just before he succumbed, a small feathered creature hopped into view. Its enormous disproportionate eyes locked on to Thorn's and then everything went black.

Archibald

The smell of sizzling bacon was the first thing Thorn noticed as he regained consciousness. The second was the warmth of a nearby fire. Snuggling the blanket tight to his chest, a loud yawn escaped for the whole world to hear. The soft fluttering of wings interrupted Thorn's peaceful slumber, followed by the small thud of something landing on his chest. Opening his eyes to a squint, a feathered face peered at him inquisitively inches away from his nose. Thorn started back and bumped his head. Behind him came a metallic noise as something dislodged and fell onto his head like a fitted headband, partially obscuring his vision.

"Hmmm... a crown? Isn't that a little ostentatious?"

The voice came from behind the fire but the glare made it hard to see who had spoken.

"I always told him honeyed bacon had the ability to wake the dead, and finally I have proof."

"Reveal yourself!" demanded Thorn.

Shuffling around the fire, a familiar face smiled with eyebrows raised high in amusement. Younger in his dream, this face was ancient but undeniably the same. Deep valleys of age wrinkled the skin of his balding head and shaking hands. In lieu of his sharp black vest and doublet, the old man now wore a tattered black monk robe fastened at the waist with a brown length of rope.

"Who are you and what the hell happened to me?" questioned Thorn.

"What do you remember?" asked the old man.

Thorn massaged his temples, closing his eyes he tried to remember how he had arrived in the temple. He pushed the crown back on his head, distracted.

"I remember a burning heat and pain… multiple levels of pain. I wanted to die. I pleaded for it." Thorn's voice shook.

The old man cackled until he saw the lack of amusement on Thorn's face.

"Oh don't be like that," said the old man, failing to hide his cheesy grin. "I find the irony amusing. To beg for death as you are being reborn, it's quite priceless if you ask me." The old man's laughter gradually subsided and he continued.

"As for who I am, you already know the answer to that, even if it eludes you at this time. Now my friend here graciously offered you some bacon and your new body will need to build up its strength."

So I was dead, thought Thorn. His chest itched at that moment, causing him to look down. The thick white scar in the center of his upper body ran the length of his rib cage. No man could survive such a wound. Pain shot through his head and memories like the links of a chain revealed themselves. So much had happened in his last day… no… not day. It had been twenty years. *The temple, silver dust, raiders... the attack, the sword, the dark men, the pain, nothingness, the ocean, the island and finally...*

"The Librarian." As Thorn mouthed the words, a piece of honeyed bacon was shoved into his mouth. Coughing, he spat it onto the ground, hissing in an agitated voice.

"Viridio don't eat meat!"

The owl watched his actions with emotion before fluttering over to the fire to retrieve another piece of bacon. He flew back landing softly on Thorn's leg and with special care placed the meat in an open hand.

"Very good, I am the Librarian. It appears most of your memories are coming back, which will help with the next step. You are more than a Viridio now, young master, and Archibald knows that. Humor him." The Librarian's bemused expression was clearly visible in the flickering firelight.

Thorn gingerly closed his fingers around the strip of bacon, eyeing the spotted tawny owl that now perched on his knee. He had seen these little birds of prey scooting around the forest on his nighttime excursions. They were no bigger than a mid-sized pumpkin and ate insects and small lizards. It was quite impressive to tame a bird of prey, no matter the size. They tended to have strong personalities.

Reluctantly, Thorn took a bite of the meat. In protest, he barely let it touch his tongue before swallowing, but this was enough to overwhelm his disgust. The oily grease filled his mouth, causing him to salivate, and Thorn was quickly overcome with ravenous hunger. Throwing his blanket off, he crawled to the fire and quickly finished off the bacon, turning his attention to a large hunk of meat roasting on a spit.

"I tried… to eat meat… once… even though it was against… Viridio customs," Thorn explained through overfull mouthfuls. "It tasted like putrid water… and made me sick for a week."

The Librarian sat back quietly while Thorn lost himself in a starved frenzy. Sucking the last scrap of meat from a well-cooked rib bone, Thorn sat back, licking juice from his fingers. The little owl hopped over to his leg, nudging a small cup of water which Thorn graciously accepted. Sipping at it, he marveled at how quickly he had grown fond of the little butler bird. Perhaps he would try training one of his own in the future. In fact Thorn felt strangely confident sitting half-naked by the cooking fire. He knew he should be wary of the unknown man and his bird, but found himself trusting them more than anyone he had ever known. He turned towards the Librarian.

"So, I know I died and I know somehow twenty years have passed, but would you please explain what exactly is going on?" He gestured at his half-clad body. "I have hair sprouting from my crotch and armpits."

The hunchbacked Librarian hobbled around the cooking fire. Gingerly, he removed the crown that had landed on Thorn's head, and tossed it to the side like spoiled fruit. As it clinked down on a nearby hill of gold, he sat down in front of Thorn, shifting around slowly until he was comfortable. The Librarian then proceeded to tell Thorn the events leading up to his death. His long narrative began with the raiders and how they had used dark magic to somehow kill off the forest's defenses. Unsure of their original intentions, the Librarian spoke of how they had imprisoned the Viridio children as slaves and sold them throughout the land. These men were from the east and were one part of three warring nations.

The Librarian had been a religious man of prestige held in high esteem by many. He had been sent a vision during his meditation and left all he knew that very same day. The vision called him to the forest exactly when the raider arrived and he had resided in the forest temple ever since.

"Twenty years with no one but Archibald to talk to. My lord provided a true test of patience."

A servant of Nemosyne, the god of memory and knowledge, it was the Librarian's job to guide Thorn through the trials and tribulations that lay ahead. It was Nemosyne who had reincarnated Thorn, but for a price. His greater purpose was still a mystery to the Librarian, but interpreting the will of a god was rarely straightforward. He only knew that Thorn had been tasked with ending a war that had been raging for centuries. Looking wistfully at the flames Thorn remembered how insignificant he had felt when facing the nothingness of a thousand voices. He shivered and goose pimples appeared on his arms and legs ignoring the warmth of the nearby cooking fire. Knowing that he now owed his life to something so powerful and beyond his understanding made Thorn queasy. Long shadows played on the walls as he collected himself. The Librarian had not stopped speaking during Thorn's momentary lapse in concentration, continuing to fill in the blanks.

"The Eastern Empire and Western Kingdoms have a fragile truce born from their mutual enemy in the north, but it decays every day. When it finally breaks, years of stockpiled hatred will spill over, soaking the world with the blood of the innocent. Your Lord requires your intervention. Only you can dispose of the warmongering individuals who have risen to power. Only you can bring peace."

The information was nothing short of overwhelming, but Thorn sat and focused, trying to remain levelheaded. He could always have a nervous breakdown later. The fire burnt low and the night turned to day, but still they talked.

"So the warm water was the sea of the dead and I gave up a part of my soul to escape it?" The questions Thorn posed seemed unending, but the Librarian didn't seem to mind. Thorn had slept for two decades. Catch up was expected.

The night had been long and filled with many answers but Thorn's curiosity was never sated. Since returning from death, his hunger seemed equally voracious. As if reading his thoughts, Archibald hopped over to present Thorn with more food.

"Yes, young master. Part of your life force was sacrificed in exchange for this second chance. I am not entirely certain, but I believe the majestic Nemosyne can bring you back as many times as needed, but like all things, it comes with a price. Your chest scar has been left to remind you of this price. No creatures of blood and bone can claim immunity from the ravages of time, save the Viridio Infinitatus. This is why you, an immortal forest child, have aged to trade life force for a second life, as it were. You now resemble a 19-year-old mortal, which explains the sudden hair growth as well as other desires you will soon discover." The Librarian finished his last sentence with a grin. Thorn rubbed his temples, saying.

"I am still having trouble remembering my time in the afterlife. It's like one of my dreams. It comes and goes in waves, strange because I can remember every word you have said since my rebirth and we have been talking for some time." The Librarian nodded sagely.

"Master Nemosyne is the god of memory and knowledge. When he returned you to this world, some of his power must have trickled over. I would not be surprised if perfect memory was but one of the many gifts you received."

"Librarian, when we were on the island you seemed different, I could barely understand what you were saying," said Thorn. The Librarian shrugged.

"Yes, I do apologize for that. My astral projected self does tend to rabble on a bit. Free of our bodies, with all their physical and mental restriction, all that remains is our true selves. Without any limitations, my true self is a bit of a know-it-all and that's putting it kindly. Now, I know you have more questions than answers, but some things can only be understood when experienced. The sun has been up for far too long and you really must get started."

The Librarian was up off the ground and tipping water over the cooking fire before Thorn even noticed. On unsteady limbs that still looked strangely big, Thorn struggled to his feet to join him. Although powerful muscles lined his new body, Thorn still felt as weak as a newborn, struggling to keep pace with the old man. In his weakened state, he could barely stand, let alone fight to save the world.

"After all the crazy things you've said, what makes you think I will do your god's dirty work? Diving straight into a war with no preparation or plan seems stupid. I don't even know where I would begin, even if I agreed to help you. Besides, I need to find someone before I agree to anything. I have tasted death once, if I have to go through hell again, I'm doing it on my terms." The Librarian stopped what he was doing and turned.

"You will do our 'dirty work' because you were chosen to do it," he said calmly, in a monotone voice, "You were not asked, but told. You will do it because you owe a debt of life that can be called in at any time. Most importantly, Thorn, you will do it because it is unwise to displease a god."

The room seemed darker than before and more menacing. It was as if the shadows had grown in size and were now paying attention to them.

"In addition," the Librarian continued cheerfully. "Helping my master will lead you to the friends that were taken, and with his help you can take them back. One in particular occupies your thoughts."

Thorn's memories of Milia serving the murderous fat man made him shudder, but also filled him with a sense of purpose.

"Okay, Librarian. You have made your point. Tell me where I can find Milia," said Thorn. "You originally said those men were from the east so that is the logical place to start looking."

As Thorn stepped forward, the Librarian caught his arm and beckoned with one finger. "In your new body you will be faster and stronger than you were before, but the journey will be long and you will need many provisions."

He dragged Thorn into a side room and pointed to a nearby table. The table was laden with many pouches filled with gold coins and gems. A burlap sack leaned against a table leg, overflowing with cured fruits and meats. Over to one side, a neatly folded black and brown tunic sat with matching trousers. The stitching gave the appearance that the material was made from bird feathers. A falcon emblem was embroidered on the chest and each shoulder.

Occupying a stand next to the table was a peculiar suit of armor unlike any Thorn had seen. In contrast to the other bulky suits found on corpses within the temple, this one was light and easy to move in.

It appeared to be comprised of mainly leather and hearth-cooled chain mail with tempered plate metal covering vital areas. Flexible seams were well-oiled to reduce friction. Although lighter than traditional western kingdom plate, Thorn could see its many advantages. Blinking back confusion, he was unsure how he knew so much about the armor's construction and effectiveness in combat. The information came unbidden as he looked at it. Evidence of a recent patching job where a small hole had been was the only damage Thorn could see.

Running his hand across the tanned leather, his fingers followed the engraved metal plate to an emblem expertly crafted at the center of the chest. It was a falcon, but unlike on the tunic, it performed a swooping dive and was circled in a golden crown. Mesmerized with the emblem, a throbbing ache began to increase at the back of Thorn's head. Unable to take his eyes off the falcon, the migraine spread throughout his head until Thorn's vision swam with lines. His breathing quickened and he could smell the smoke of houses burning. The clashing of steel could be heard in the distance whilst women cried for their children.

An Old Life

Knight General Patterson was barking orders, randomly throwing assignments to any soldier that passed him. Avion city was going to fall, this was plain to see, but not before one last push. The Knight General did his best to bolster morale in his soldiers, but he knew they were all dead men. It was just a matter of time.

Knight General Patterson noticed one of his elite watching the chaos and strode towards him.

"Captain Hughes, walk with me." Hughes took up pace next to the Knight General, listening intently.

"Captain, our city is lost. Somehow these bastards opened the outer defenses in the night. I'm leading the last of our men out to slow the Gworlug tribesmen down. Hopefully this will give the royals and civilians time to evacuate. I need you to head to Golden Ring Hospital and get my son out. I know he is sickly, but I would rather he die running than at the hands of the Gworlug. Their treatment of newborns is known to you and it will not happen to my child".

"Yes, sir," said Captain Hughes. Patterson noted the trepidation in the Captain's response.

"Hughes, you are one of the last members of our Old Falcon Guard. I know you will protect my son as if he were royalty. Make your way to the Marabela River and take a small boat down to Grasston near The Infinity Forest. There you will find a sect of holy men I have contacted. They may be able to heal him. He is the last of my line and must follow in my footsteps."

The Knight General clapped Hughes on the shoulder before turning away to order the advance. Without another word, he joined a squad to march down the causeway.

Captain Hughes regretted he could not follow his friend and mentor into battle for the last time, but accepted his orders without question. The outer defenses had fallen to utter silence. Someone on the inside must have let the Gworlug in, Hughes thought to himself. As much as he hated it, he was well-versed in subterfuge. It always ruined a fair fight. The Old Falcon Guard had been created to root out all known threats to the royal family. They required a deep understanding of espionage and assassination plots. Spies and assassins rarely fought face-to-face and with a tough military upbringing Captain Hughes would pick a duel over shady back-handed dealings every time.

His training told him there must be traitors within the Avion Guard ranks. How far the rot had spread was unknown, but it was there. The Gworlug tribesmen were stupid brutes, utterly obsessed with base pleasures and killing. There was no way they could have bypassed the outer scouting perimeter, let alone breach the city, without assistance. After one hundred years of war, the Old Falcon Guards were just too few in number to sniff out every threat. They had been a noble order in the beginning but never-ending war had taken its toll. Many had given their lives for the kingdom. The bulk of the Old Falcon Guard now served as overqualified bodyguards to the royal family. If all went as planned, those on duty had moved the royals to security vault six in the eastern wing of the palace. From there, the royal family could escape through the myriad of tunnels that went well outside the city walls.

No man could be spared in the defense of the Avion, so Captain Hughes set off alone. Adopting a low profile, he made his way towards the center of the city using backstreets and alleyways. It may not have been the most direct route, but it would be the least populated. Every unsuspecting Gworlug scout Hughes encountered was quickly dispatched with a dirk to the neck. He moved fast. Face-to-face confrontations took time and the child needed his protection.

The gleaming arches of Golden Ring Hospital came into view as Hughes exited any alleyway. Entering the large structure, it was clear that terror ran rampant. People shoved and pushed, knocking each other down in an attempt to evacuate loved ones. Bare steel was shown, glittering with threats. Fear was the meal of the day and everyone partook their fill. Referred to as bear boy in his youth, Captain Hughes was not a small man, but it required every ounce of his weight and size to act as a battering ram, clearing a path to the registration desk. Skinny noblemen flew as he plowed through the throng. A little golden ring nurse saw him approaching, recognized him and shouted.

"He's in Room 124! Take the herbs on the table next to him. He will need them!"

Nodding curtly, Hughes climbed the stairs to the infant ward and started counting room numbers. Reaching 124, he practically ripped the door off its hinges charging into the room. Two ring nurses greeted him with fear-filled expressions until they saw the swooping falcon on his chest. Knight General Patterson had sent a runner moments after the war bell had rung, telling them to prepare his son for travel, they said. They could not condone moving the child, but it was not their place to argue.

"The boy is weak, my Lord. Without proper medical care, he will not last a week," said one ring nurse.

"If he stays in this city, he will not see tomorrow's sun rise," said Captain Hughes. "You have done all you can for him. Please find a place to hole up. Avion City has fallen. If you hide, you may be spared the worst of it."

The women would not heed his warning, Hughes knew. They would remain in the hospital, tending the sick until they were found by the Gworlug. They would be raped and murdered, but not necessarily in that order. Hughes scooped up the tightly swaddled infant along with a pouch of herbs and left the room, filled with pity. Unsheathing his great sword, he left the hospital the same way he had entered. This time, however, the tide of frightened noblemen parted to let him through. His face displayed his desire to kill.

As he left the hospital, Hughes turned down one of the many adjacent side streets just as a wail came from behind him. Screams of terror echoed from Golden Ring hospital. The Gworlug Tribesmen had made their way already. It would be a massacre. The need to protect rose up in him like bitter bile in his throat. Hughes looked down at the child in his arms, remembered his promise, and turned in the direction of the docks. The screams chased him with every step.

Ducking through alleyways and abandoned buildings, Hughes avoided detection. His long sword was unsheathed, resting comfortably on one shoulder and prepared to silence any threat. Luckily, he knew the city well and made it to the river district without incident. There, he found that mercenaries had already locked down the main docks whilst boatloads of Gworlug Tribesmen disembarked.

Hughes cursed lightly under his breath and performed a cursory count. *For this number of enemies to occupy the docks, they had to have arrived hours ago, yet no alarm had been raised and no dead bodies marked resistance. Every guard post within the river district had a warning bell, yet none had rung. In addition, all defensive gates were open and unmarked. It was just not possible, yet here was the evidence right before his eyes.*

Hugging the shadows, Hughes knew there was no chance of avoiding detection if he simply attempted to sail. The Gworlug would riddle him with arrows the moment he attempted to take a ship. He would need a distraction that would hold their attention.

"When behind enemy lines nothing draws attention like a threatening blaze," whispered Hughes, remembering his grizzled drill instructor's experienced words.

Returning to the alleyways Captain Hughes entered a familiar tanning hut through its open window. If he lived through this, he would have to thank Paddy the oil merchant with a fat kiss and a tankard. Hugging a large barrel of tanning oil to his chest, Hughes left the same way he had entered and found his next obstacle only a short jaunt down the road. He wrestled with the sloshing contents until they were firmly pinned beneath one arm and began his ascent. *The ladder creaked and moaned beneath the combined weight of man and cask but held firm long enough for Hughes to reach the rooftops. Breathing hard Hughes stretched his taxed muscles for a moment before plunging his dirk into the soft wooden barrel. Stab, twist, pull, stab, twist, pull, by the time the dirk returned to its sheath the barrel had so many holes the contents threatened to flood. Hughes had to move fast to coat the required rooftops. The flint and steel were in his hands before he could comprehend the carnage soon to follow.*

"Hopefully everyone is out."

The fire engulfed two buildings before Hughes could blink, traveling on the tanning oil he had drenched the rooftops with. Towers of flame reached for the sky, advertising their presence with belching columns of black smoke. The poor quarter nestled against the docks and was mostly deserted. Poor craftsmanship and cheap wooden frames made every house a tinderbox only requiring a spark for his purpose. The tanning oil was overkill, but Hughes had no room for failure.

Satisfied with his timing, he slipped by a group of Gworlug at the outer edges of the docks, praying the sick child in his arms would remain silent. Their attention was fixed on the pillars of fire and the frantic efforts of those trying to stop it from spreading. Carefully placing the child in a small boat furthest from the action, Hughes untied the mooring line and cast off. Keeping the sail down to avoid detection, he rowed slowly towards an aqueduct that connected to the Marabela River. His plan seemed to have worked and Hughes relaxed into the rhythm of a steady row. Suddenly, pain erupted in his shoulder with a crunching thud. Seconds later arrows hissed by the boat. Turning to face their origin, Hughes grabbed a crate lid as a makeshift shield and sheltered the boy. Two arrows bit into the wood inches from his face. On the shore, Hughes could now see the Gworlug massing.

Luckily the current had picked up and in a short few seconds the boat would be obscured from view. Noticing movement on a nearby rooftop, Hughes spied a dark figure aiming a large crossbow and raised his shield arm. The bolt splintered his makeshift shield, and buried itself deep in the boat deck behind him. Hughes felt winded, doubling over he tried desperately to breathe. His hand moved over his stomach and he could feel the hole punched in the plate armor. The bolt had left a gaping hole in his abdomen, passing cleanly through. Never before had Hughes seen an armor-piercing bolt so effective at such a distance. There had only been time for one shot, but that's all it took. The boat moved to cover, entering the mouth of the aqueduct, as Hughes fumbled with the straps at his shoulders. Undoing several more clasps, his armor dropped to the deck, coated with a thick layer of blood. If he could not stop the bleeding, his mission would fail and the boy would die alongside him.

Passing in and out of consciousness, Hughes attempted to steer his vessel towards the village of Grasston. After compressing the wound, Hughes soaked rags with alcohol from his trusty flask and secured them with repurposed armor straps. Erecting the small vessel's sail depleted what little energy he had left. Small jerks in the rudder would occasionally wake him long enough to feed the child herbs before he passed out again. The Marabela River flowed deep and wide, but as the boat neared the Infinity forest, navigation required a fully conscious mind. Smaller rivers flowed from the mighty Marabela and many led to swampland or lakes further downstream. The trick was staying as far to the west of the river as possible, but his blood loss was making it hard to concentrate.

Coming to for a moment, Hughes smiled as he spotted one of the Grasston mills. Whether it was dumb luck, superior navigating or divine intervention, he had almost made it. Closing his eyes in an attempt to conserve energy, Hughes prayed silently for the strength to finish his mission and deliver the child in one piece. The monks knew what was needed to heal the child but if he sailed past Grasston Village or died, it wouldn't matter who eventually found them. The boy had one dose of medicine left and was running short on time. Nearly there, Hughes closed his eyes in relief.

The boat rumbled as the hull slid onto land, forcing Hughes to begrudgingly open his eyes. A structure the likes of which he had never seen stood towering over the boat. The river ran directly into the building lapping at mismatched stone walls. West and Eastern architecture were only two of the styles that made up this madman's dream. Forest surrounded the boat and the strange building as far as the eye could see. He had failed. Somewhere on the outskirts of Grasston, the river must have forked towards the Infinity forest and led the boat here. He had not been strong enough to stay awake.

Gathering the child, Hughes clambered off of the boat into the cool water which was only knee-deep. Shaking off the head spin and blurred vision, he stumbled in the direction of the large building's door. Every breath was a labor and every step threatened to collapse his knees beneath him. Finally, unable to continue, Hughes saw the ground rushing to meet him. He had been only steps from the entrance. The child was crying now, the first sounds it had made since leaving the city. Through darkening vision, Hughes saw an old man dressed in monk's robes emerge from the doorway. Hughes forced his lungs to push breath a final time.

"You must save the child."

The old man squatted down, scooping Patterson's son up effortlessly and looked at Hughes without expression.

"I will do all I can, sir. Rest and recover your strength."

Hughes closed his eyes and all remained dark.

A New Life

The wet towel on Thorn's head sent droplets of water down the sides of his neck making him shiver.

"So now I have the nightmares when I'm awake... Fantastic," he said to himself.

Thorn woke from his dreams to a spinning world that slowly solidified. He lay on the floor, a small distance from the armor that had sparked his waking nightmare. It was unclear how much time had passed since his collapse, but it was long enough for someone to prop his head up with a pillow and place a blanket over his chest. *Most likely the Librarian,* thought Thorn. Sitting up, Thorn called to the old man several times, but received no answer. He was either out of earshot or had left to gather provisions.

"Geez, I'm hungry again. Why does this new body need so much food? Useless."

In response to Thorn's words, a flutter in the air preceded Archibald landing on his knee with several pieces of bacon.

"Why thank you, Archi. You're the best helper I have ever had. But don't let Milia know, you might find yourself baked into a pie." Having not met Milia, the small bird took Thorn's attempt at humor seriously, and with an indignant glare left in search of more food.

After eating his fill, Thorn felt some of his strength returning and his eyes once again moved to the armor with the diving falcon. *The Old Falcon Guard.* Hughes and Patterson were both high-ranking members. Two of Thorn's most vivid dreams had revolved around that order of Knights. The first time he was Knight General Patterson a man past his prime but clearly idolized by all of his men. Much of what happened to Patterson could only be remembered as blurred after images. The second time, as Captain Hughes, however all memories remained as clear as crystal rock. The armor the men wore, the swords they fought with—even the faces of the innocent as they ran in terror. It was no longer a dream. It was a different reality, filled with other men's thoughts, feelings and emotions.

Crawling over to the armor, Thorn inspected where the dream crossbow bolt had hit Hughes. Sure enough, there was a scar in the metal where a well-skilled smith had mended the hole. So, the dreams were actually memories, memories of dead men. Then that meant every nightmare Thorn had ever had of violent death, strange places and beasts might actually have been visions of past events. Up until now, all of the stories had been jumbled and fragmented. Thorn would see a bird in the sky or the shape in a tree, and be vaguely reminded of something that had never happened to him. Before, he had always shrugged this off as an active imagination, but ever since he had come back from death's doorstep the stories started to categorize in his mind. Upon seeing Captain Hughes' damaged armor, the mélange of memories bubbled to the surface with all the emotion and pain that accompanied them.

This explained much of Thorn's life. Of course he was an outsider in a single-minded community, he was a creature of many minds. Thorn had hundreds, if not thousands, of outsider memories floating around in his head. Always questioning authority, and understanding that a soothsayer was such a weak political position. Even barons and kings were beneath emperors and tribal leaders of other continents and the separation grew even more when you looked at gods and otherworldly things. He had not simply been lucky when attacking the slavers all those years ago. It had been the reactions and techniques of warriors, lives already lived. Armed with snippets of fighting knowledge and a child's body, Thorn had cut down all in his way until the man in black had killed him. Flexing his hand into a fist, tight sinewy muscle rippled across his forearm. *Next time will be different,* thought Thorn.

The world had suddenly opened up and the gravity of his current circumstances finally dawned. He had inadvertently become a god's champion or at the very least he was in the deity Nemosyne's debt. He would repay the debt and try his absolute best to complete the task set before him, but first he needed to finish what he started the day he had died. Thorn was already twenty years late to save Milia and the other Viridio from slavery and death. They had waited long enough.

Thorn moved over to the table and dressed in the clothing that had been laid out prior to his vision. Remembering the correct sequence of clasps and straps, he fastened the armor on over his tunic, enjoying the weight of the metal and leather. If he was a little larger in the chest and shoulders it would make a perfect fit. A few aggressive adjustments and tightened straps made the suit very manageable. As he gathered the provisions from the table, Thorn noticed a piece of parchment recently scrawled upon.

Thorn,

I have equipped you with everything you need to begin the mission my master has entrusted to you. I apologize for leaving without a farewell but I had pressing business and was unsure how long your mind would need to process the soldier's memories.

I know you will first attempt to rescue your people from the slavers we discussed earlier. My master will allow this. It may prove an excellent learning experience and will certainly clear your mind for what is to come. You are as much a servant of Nemosyne as I am. He will guide your hand to purpose, no matter how hard you resist. So don't resist. Head west to the town of Grasston when you leave this temple. There you will find monks of our order. They will point you in the right direction.

The armor that I assume you now wear is a relic of a bygone era and has a fierce reputation. If you let it, that armor will open many doors for you in the future, so use it to your best advantage.

I leave you with one final thought. You have been blessed with knowledge from the Master, but in essence, knowledge is not power but a commodity. Power is gained by knowledge withheld. If I tell all around me the secrets that I possess, I bring myself to their level. Only through withholding that information do I become superior.

Yours Cordially,
The Librarian
Humble Servant of the MASTER NEMOSYNE

PS. I did all I could to help Captain Hughes and his child but in the end it was not enough. Wear the boy's bracelet in remembrance—it may bring you luck.

Lifting the parchment, Thorn found a silver bracelet hiding beneath. It was quite simple in its construction, solid and practical. Four small topaz jewels sat evenly spaced around its face at four opposite ends. Inside the bracelet opposite the jewels were engraved the letters N,S,E, and W, like a compass. Thorn stared at the engraving, searching his memories, and suddenly was looking through the eyes of Knight General Patterson.

The Knight General had not been present during his son's birth. The campaign in the east had taken up much of his time. The bracelet was given to the child the first time his father had laid eyes on him.

Thorn slid on the hunk of silver and gathered the rest of his things. Making his way to the exit, Thorn enjoyed the familiar yet strange feel of the armor as it followed his movements. The weight and sense of protection were good, but something was amiss. The empty space on his hip was the problem. Strange as it was to have outsider comforts and routines bubble to the surface of his consciousness, Thorn agreed that he would need a weapon for his journey. Walking over to the dark marble altar he had once used to create the magical silver sand, Thorn grabbed an ornamental dagger from a nearby pile of gold. He sliced the blade into his hand, deep enough for a good flow of blood.

Strange words issued from his lips, unbidden, as he recited a prayer in an ancient tongue. The blood dripped into the basin, creating crimson rivulets on the altar's surface. He prayed on, his own mind uncomprehending the actions of his tongue. Past experience suggested running was a good idea, but the heat from his previous attempts never came. Sparks and steam rose from the altar, but the display was rather unimpressive and nothing like the pyrotechnics of the past. Steam cleared, slowly revealing the pile of silver sand he had purchased with his blood. Using this sand, Thorn had once created a sword from memories and nothingness. This was something he wished to see again. As his freshest memories were of Captain Hughes, Thorn pictured the Captain's sword and held it in his mind. Using his bloodied hand to grab a handful of shining dust, he threw it into the air.

The sand flew into a high-forming cloud as Thorn focused on the sword's craftsmanship. No detail was forgotten. The keenly sharpened tip that had pierced flesh and steel relentlessly for ten years, the nicks and scrapes of one hundred battles, the sheath that had once knocked out two unlucky smugglers when they decided to renege on a deal—the sword remained in Thorn's mind until it became a reality. Producing a small shimmer of light, the dust rearranged in the air, becoming solid. It dropped into Thorn's waiting hands as a fully formed weapon and sheath.

Drawing the blade and feeling its weight, Thorn now realized how crude his last attempt to construct a weapon had been, accidental as it was. Now Thorn had much more control. He still did not know what this silver sand was, but he would find out from the Librarian or the monks in Grasston. The Librarian had called them part of "our order." As such, they would have to answer his questions and assist in travel preparation.

Thorn attached the sword to his hip with efficiency practiced in dreams and emptied a money pouch to scoop up the remaining silver dust. It was a precious commodity and Thorn had a sneaking suspicion he would not find its equal anywhere else in the world. Archi the owl had been sitting quietly, watching events unfold. He had perched safely on a nearby banister, but with two flaps he silently glided to the exit, screeching as he landed. Thorn agreed with his sentiments.

"Yes, yes, I agree, Archi. It is time for me to go. You're just as impatient as the Librarian. You don't have to worry. Soon you will have the temple all to yourself."

Thorn had to duck to exit the temple's secret door. To his surprise, the small owl followed, gliding across the meadow to perch in a large tree. Thorn stood atop the temple, gazing across the Forbidden Meadow.

He had died as an outcast child of the forest. He would leave it as something else: a weapon shaped by memory, bound by debt, and pointed east. Somewhere beyond the trees, Milia was waiting. Somewhere beyond her, the men who had taken her still breathed. Thorn intended to correct both problems.

The forest looked almost unchanged, but Thorn knew Milia would not be so lucky. More than twenty years had passed. Twenty years in chains.

Twenty years at the mercy of the monster from his vision.

Don't worry, Milia, Thorn thought. *I'm coming for you.*

For Authors: Authortunities

Authortunities is a weekly calendar newsletter designed specifically for writers to find all the author opportunities they need in a single, curated format. Open submission calls, contests, workshops, open mics, grants and more, in your inbox every Saturday.

Organized by emoji, *Authortunities* contains four weeks of valuable opportunities for authors. Enjoy the next two weeks of opportunities at no cost. Access the entire four weeks of opportunities for just $5.55 a month.

However you take advantage of it, your *Authortunities* are waiting for you.

https://authortunities.substack.com/freemonth

Exercise your writes. Get published. Make change.

Did you enjoy Thorn?

Word-of-mouth recommendations and online reviews help new readers discover the Shadow's Lament series. If Thorn pulled you into the forest, the temple, or the war beyond, please consider leaving a short review at your favorite bookseller or library website.

About the Author

Ryan Aussie Smith is an Australian author, voice actor, and publisher with a lifelong love of fantasy, gaming, mythology, and character-driven adventure. His fiction blends dark humor, strange magic, brutal worlds, and reluctant heroes thrown into impossible circumstances. He is also co-publisher and audio producer for *Space & Time* magazine, in continuous print since 1966.

You can connect with me on:

- https://www.twitch.tv/aussiemanplays
- https://x.com/RyanAussieSmith
- https://www.facebook.com/profile.php?id=100004086123943

Subscribe to my newsletter:

- https://authortunities.substack.com

www.ingramcontent.com/pod-product-compliance
Lightning Source LLC
LaVergne TN
LVHW010941110826
845149LV00013B/2711

* 9 7 8 1 9 5 9 0 4 8 2 1 3 *